Inside~
Outside

Stories

Regi Claire

SCOTTISH CULTURAL PRESS

EDINBURGH

First published in 1998 by
Scottish Cultural Press
14/130 Leith Walk
Edinburgh EH6 5DT
Tel: 0131 555 5950
e-mail: scp@sol.co.uk
http://www.taynet.co.uk/users/scp

ISBN: 1 84017 023 9

The publisher acknowledges subsidy from

THE SCOTTISH ARTS COUNCIL

towards the publication of this book

Printed and bound by Cromwell Press Ltd., Trowbridge, Wiltshire

for Ron and Klara, forever

Acknowledgements

Many thanks are due to the editors of the following publications in which some of these stories previously appeared – initially under the pen name Yvonne D. Claire:

Chapman 85; *Edinburgh Review* 95, 97 and 99; *New London Writers* 3; *Northwords* 9 and 15; *Quality Women's Fiction* 13; *Shorts: The Macallan/Scotland on Sunday Short Story Collection* (Polygon); *Marilynre várva: Mai skót novellák* (Hungary); and *Unu* 7.7-8 (Romania).

Heartfelt thanks go to my husband and to Gavin for believing in me even when I had lost faith; to Roger and to my family in Switzerland for their enthusiasm and encouragement; and, last but not least, to Ruth for my first 'real' books.

I am very grateful to the Scottish Arts Council for a Writer's Bursary which allowed me to complete this collection in my own space and time.

Contents

Over, All Over and Beyond

'*Ecoute*,' I said, 'listen, don't do that.' I kicked him, not too hard, and moved away towards the other end of the bar. Next thing I knew he'd scrambled to his feet from where he'd been groping about on the floor, looking up my skirt, and was following me, slowly, his face closed-up and dark, a hunter's face, his right hand clenched into a fist. I almost tripped over the legs of one of the stools and steadied myself against the rail that ran along the counter:

'Felix, please, he's going to –'

Felix didn't even lift his head, just squinted at the glass he'd been polishing, twirling it in his fingers. The man was almost up against me now. I tried to back away, but I'd reached the wall.

'*Tu vois ça*? Yes?' His fist coming closer; inch by inch he was raising his fist towards me, with the deadly concentration of a drunk. A smell, acrid and overpowering, monkey hairs on knuckles. I wanted to throw up my arms and push him away, I wanted to scream, toss my head. Instead, something pierced the small of my neck –

I was sitting on the floor, propped up against the bar, and Felix was pouring cold water over me. My neck hurt, and I felt a little dazed.

'Better?' Felix asked, dangling the empty pitcher.

I managed a grin, 'Hmm, thanks. You got a spare towel by any chance?'

Someone touched my shoulder: '*Vois donc*, please you see ...' The voice stung me to the quick. What was *he* still doing here? Had no one called the police?

I struggled to get up when suddenly a fist swung in front of my eyes. Fingers began to unclasp and there, cutting grimy rings into the flesh, lay several coins on an open palm. 'You see,' the hand shook slightly, 'always it has money under bar. I find. For beer, *tu vois*?' He laughed, loud and happy, while behind him on the wall a large sea urchin swayed to and fro, to and fro, for no reason at all.

I could have cried like a child.

Meanwhile Ramon would be jabbering away at one of his interminable conferences I'd given up accompanying him to. South Africa this time: far, so far. He was never around when I needed him. That was the first lesson I'd learnt in the four months of our marriage.

I went and stood on the terrace. The sea breeze had died down, and the air pressed into me thick and silent, as cloying as candyfloss. Two dogs were chasing each other along the curve of the lagoon, dodging the sweaty tourists draped on their hotel towels like offerings. Every so often, the smaller, fawn-coloured one would roll over and lie completely still, its throat turned towards the glint of the other's teeth.

A shame their fight wasn't for real. The island was rampant with those skinny strays. Worse than the cockroaches they were. Howling and scavenging and copulating all over the place. Giving birth in the cemetery. Giving birth non-stop, it seemed, until their teats were ragged and trailing in the dirt. Later you'd come across them by the roadside, even the male dogs bloated now and breeding . . . whatever. Blowflies. New life.

Ramon always said I wouldn't have any problems finding a job as an English teacher down here: 'Of course not, with your qualifications, your experience.' Sometimes he made it sound more like a question; he wasn't a native speaker, after all. I still had my Girl-Guide enthusiasm then and wanted to believe such reassurances, whispers so silky soft and phosphorescent they spin a cocoon around you until –

Snap! You wake up, all alone, and it's night, and there's a storm going on, drowning the prowl of footsteps outside. The muddy footprints are washed away again by the rain. Apart from one – which you discover

*next morning, just beside the back door, when you check the bungalow and
garden for storm damage.*

A gust of wind had risen from the spiky green stillness of the
sugar-cane fields beyond the village, lifting my T-shirt, still wet
from Felix's pitcher, and slapping it against my belly, hard, almost
viciously. The flame-breasted bird that had been sipping drops of
water from an aircon pipe nearby flew up in a fright. The land
breeze had started, it would be dark soon. I picked up my bag and
went down the steps, down and away to where the beach was
empty, walking quite slowly to feel the sand sifting through my
toes.

I avoided the hotels and gave Coom at the boat-house,
gap-toothed Coom with his skin the colour of scorched wood
and as brittle, a wave instead. Only today I was being stupid,
thoughtless really, because he waved back and there was
something in his hand. I shielded my eyes from the glare. A flipper.
He was brandishing a flipper. He was hitting out at the distance
between us, smacking it, shouting words in Creole. My heart
tightened and my hand fell stiffly to my side as I carried on, a
little faster now. What was he doing that for? Another game of
hide and seek *à la mauricienne*? The longer you lived on this island,
the less you understood, and the less you . . . I held my breath,
stunned: Or did Coom *know* about the footprint outside the
bungalow? Did he . . . ? Had he . . . ? Inside me was a heap of
scree someone had trodden on.

At first I thought I was going to be sick and dropped on all
fours, panting. But nothing happened, except that for a while I
couldn't see anything; it was like snow blindness in a country
without snow. Once the grains of sand and tiny shells had
trickled back where they belonged, I got up. The tide was out
and the rocks lay hunched in the shallows, fuzzy shapes, barely
under the surface. If you went too close, the coral that bristled all
over their shoulders, nasty brown coral like the matted hair of a

giant, would etch blood lines on your skin. The water had lost its pre-storm clearness; it had a murky, troubled look, as if thousands of sea cucumbers were steaming away furiously.

Nowhere was safe ground any more. How could I make Ramon understand? He who'd studied law and firmly believed you couldn't lose your footing as long as you kept within certain boundaries, boundaries staked out by the society you were part of. Which society was I part of anyway? In the mud just in front of me were my own marks, nicely symmetrical, from toes, knees and spread hands, two adjoining squares, like cages.

Even the Dundee Lion had stopped being neutral territory, with its drunks creeping and crawling around the bar stools in the half-light, scaring off the other customers. When all I'd hoped for was to meet some expats, feel their sympathy. Felix was British, of course, but I didn't want to tell *him*; he wasn't really the type to share confidences with.

I turned to go, then suddenly found myself facing the sea again, crouching now, and my fingers were grubbing and clawing into the sand, hurling it away by the fistful: angry, spluttering arches of dirt right over the marks I'd made – over, all over and beyond.

Finally, I set off towards the road and the bungalow's cunning system of padlocks.

Ever since school through to university and teacher training college I seemed to have gone for men whose names started with 'M'. So why I've ended up with Ramon I'm not sure. Unless it's because he's Mauritian and his surname's Mitchell. Occasionally, just as a joke, I make up anagrams: when I'm in a cold and windy mood I call him Moran, for its Scottish ring; when I feel hot and barbarous he becomes Maron, which I pronounce with double 'r', like the French for 'chestnut' – after all, his skin's as brown and shinily smooth. Ramon doesn't mind, at least not in private. In public, of course, he is lawyer Ramon Mitchell, with a degree from Oxford and a bank account in Switzerland, smug and slightly arrogant.

We'd met on the Edinburgh–Glasgow train early one Friday evening about a year ago. He'd just got himself a cup of coffee from the trolley, and the vendor wouldn't accept his twenty: 'New regulations, I'm afraid; all those forgeries . . .' I sat watching them act it out in the darkness of the window, feeling high as a kite after a few end-of-the-week drinks with some colleagues. Well, I had plenty of loose change on me, so what the hell – I gestured to the woman, then smiled at him across two empty rows of seats.

The sun was almost touching the horizon by now, its rays slanting pale and yellow through the feathery leaves of the filao trees by the beach. It sank much more rapidly out here than at home, or what I used to call home – because I was at home here now, wasn't I? – so rapidly that nightfall still caught me by surprise sometimes, like a door being shut in my face. I walked faster; I had to get back to the bungalow before dark. My bag was knocking against my hip with every step, and inside the bag was the jingling. Always the jingling. I imagined the keys, the metal blistery and greasy from the heat, sliding about on the ring, twisting, their bits touching, then gripping and hooking into each other, barely long enough, before clattering apart to start all over again. Damn those keys, the whole frigging bunch of them.

I clamped the bag under my arm and hurried on. To my left, a cock began to screech behind the corrugated-iron fencing round a shack and a banana tree, and I nearly stumbled over the hen that came rushing through a gap squawking and flailing its wings.

Before we bought our wedding rings I'd said to Ramon: 'But I'll never be a submissive wife, even living in the Indian Ocean won't change that. You'd better warn your mother straightaway.'

He stared at me for a moment, his eyes black and glittering as a gecko's, then he began to laugh. Soon he was rocking and roaring with laughter. He laughed so much his face puckered up into a crisscross of lines and I had to slap him on the back: 'Ha-ha-harder,' he gasped, 'come on, harder . . .'

What on earth was the matter with him? I hadn't meant to be funny. And my hand was getting sore too, as if his spine was making gashes into it.

All of a sudden he fell quiet, pulled me close. 'Don't worry,' he said, stroking my cheeks and down to what he calls the 'bird's belly' under my chin, 'she'll be expecting that. There won't be any reading of sheets after *our* wedding night . . .'

The palm of my hand was marbled red and white. I tried not to swallow, waiting for the pain to ease off.

Across the street, the road workers I'd passed earlier were leaning against the wall of a shop that doubled as a bar, drinking.

'*Ça va?*' they called out in their strange singsong.

I hesitated, '*Oui, ça va bien.*' I never quite knew how to behave in a situation like this – whether to simply ignore people or nod, smile even; whether to greet them.

'*Hé, hé!*' One of the workers was gesturing with his bottle of Phoenix Beer. When he saw me looking, he took a swig, licked the froth off his lips and cried, 'Ah! Ah! AAAH!'

The others started laughing.

I could have spat at them. Had they, too, heard I was alone out there, at the bungalow? Who would have told them, though? My face was wetter than ever, streaming with sweat. Why was everybody trying to frighten me? It wasn't my fault I still hadn't found a job, still wasn't earning any money. Why were they all cutting the ground from under my feet, hacking it up into clods, then half-clods, finally crumbs and grit? Quicksands. Already the colours were fading into shadows. A few more minutes and it would be night, pitch-black night.

It wasn't much further now. But what then? What was I to do? Perhaps if I managed to get hold of Ramon he'd try to re-route his flight and return a day or two early. If I explained about the footprint, surely he'd understand. Because he'd rung only yesterday, before the storm, to ask how I was. 'So-so,' I'd said in my brightest voice, guilty at making him feel guilty and yet wanting him to feel the weight.

The deserted bungalow − Every gate along the street reminded me, every door. And beyond the gates, the doors −

Well, nothing. Don't be silly. Nothing except the cockroaches holed up in their crevices or scuttling in cupboards and behind the cooker; and the geckos, of course, all turquoise and emerald and jade, amiably slinking up to yet another insect then, afterwards, spurting yet another mural. Remember how you secured and snibbed, how you bolted, locked and fastened yourself out of that bungalow, all the way from the rooftop down to the spiderwebbed larder window in the basement? You checked and double-checked. That in itself was pretty ridiculous, let's be honest. For it was outside *you'd found the footprint. One single footprint outside a door you'd kept religiously locked. Could be you'd forgotten about the gate, left it open, and some tramp wandered in to shelter from the bad weather. So you went and matched up traces of mud on the veranda till you had convinced yourself, worked yourself up into a state.*

But I used not to be like that. I used not to be afraid of things before. Not even of the Northern dark in the city with its shadows falling across doorways, blanketing empty spaces. And certainly not of a dark like this, a dark full of sunheat and laughter and the sounds of the ocean against the reef . . .

A group of people have emerged from the well-lit apartment block ahead. For an instant the wind's afloat with scraps of conversation, shouts, the slam of car doors, an engine starting up. Seconds later their headlights are in my eyes and the night shatters, then re-forms. A few houses away the giant banyan tree, its roots and branches all tangled up and entwined, is a looming blackness. After the tree I'll have to take the dirt road −

Maybe I shouldn't go back to the bungalow and just ring Ramon from here; there's a payphone over at Ali's grocery store. But I don't have his number. It's on a slip of paper somewhere in that twilight kitchen slashed by shadows . . . Who else −? How about Kistna for a change? Kistna, my good old mother-in-law, and yet almost a stranger. She'll be so glad to hear from me. She'll ask lots of questions and talk freely. And if I tell her of the footprint, she'll do her best to help.

I'm about to cross when a dog breaks into a howling bark nearby. Its fierceness snaps at me, rips right into me. Yes, Kistna will do her very best. She'll be only too anxious to help. In tones as slithery as her saris she'll dish out her warnings, speak of wifely duties, of strength and endurance. Lovingly she'll feed my fears, pat them into place. Damn her.

But that leaves only the beach. No, more than that: the strays, the sea. Me and the sea and the strays and the beach. Perhaps the moon. Yes, the moon, too. All the stars even.

And such a sight it will be: the ocean whip-lashed into froth rearing up snorting and kicking against the barrier and tearing off bits of coral bones spitting them across into the lagoon and the lagoon itself in a bile-coloured frenzy with coconuts tossing and clashing on the waves like dead men's heads −

~

Kalsang's Brother

Miss Robinson is four foot ten, with sharp lime-green eyes and a voice like a metal spoon scraping out one of her saucepans. No matter how loud the hiss of frying fat or water boiling over, she can always make herself heard. Nothing escapes her notice: two sprinklings of pepper instead of one, and her girls are in for a lecture on the effects of 'too much spice'.

Not that Miss Robinson's had a taste of the real spice of life so far; that, unfortunately, has never yet come her way. Still, there's nothing obviously wrong with her: she looks sturdy enough, her hair is a natural pale yellow, the kind that doesn't grey easily, and when she smiles, which is not too often and more like a glare, her teeth are unexpectedly white and even.

In her heart of hearts she longs for someone to sweep her off the painstakingly polished floor-tiles of the domestic science kitchen and carry her away, but as soon as she finds herself in company, whether male or female, she feels so terribly, terribly small that her tone invariably grows shrill and virginally abrasive. Sometimes in class, before allowing the girls to sit down to their jointly produced meals, she stares at them and announces, scouring-strength, how she doesn't want them to gorge themselves and that they must learn to stop at the point where they can still force down a slice of stale bread.

It's Wednesday, 10.17 a.m. by the staff-room clock. Miss Robinson is bracing herself for another showdown with the new bunch of thirteen-year-olds she was assigned a few weeks ago, in mid-term. By the time she rinses out her cup her breath has a bitter flare to it that's not entirely due to the coffee.

The door of her classroom is closed, but the girls inside are quite definitely *not* copying down the recipes written on the board for their lesson. They're talking. Talking in shrieks and giggles, and Miss Robinson has no difficulty picturing them lolling around the tables that double as desks, shaking their hair out over the clean formica surfaces, filing and polishing nails, and nonchalantly flicking off dead bits of skin. She herself is very neat and tidy and would never dream of making her *toilette* anywhere except a bathroom, and then only bent over the wash-hand basin.

She grits her teeth, about to press down the doorhandle, when she hears one of the girls say 'Kalsang's brother' in a loud, excited-sounding voice. Miss Robinson hesitates. She has recognised the speaker and is appalled by the intensity of her enthusiasm. Surely, whether Kalsang has a brother or not would seem the least of Edith's worries – thin and bony Edith, who'd do much better to spend her surplus energy on eating up her food for a change. But Miss Robinson's curiosity has been whetted. Kalsang, after all, is the most unsettling creature she's come across in the nineteen years of her teaching career. Descended from Tibetan refugees who founded a colony in one of the neighbouring villages, this particular thirteen-year-old has grown up hard and sinuous and inscrutably superior, just like her name. So now there is a brother, too ... If nothing else, it's Miss Robinson's duty to find out more. Stooping slightly, she leans forward –

'Oh, hello Miss. Sorry we're late. There were queues at the checkouts.'

Miss Robinson spins round, draws herself up with a gasp and darts furious glances at the three girls who've caught her lingering beside her own door, five minutes after the bell has rung. Sonja and Angela, the two Italians, are holding up their carrier bags on angled arms, awkwardly, like shields; Kalsang stands behind them, eyes gleaming in the wooden darkness of her face, waiting, and very, very tall. For several seconds nobody speaks. Then Miss Robinson reaches out for their shopping:

'Well, at last. I hope you haven't forgotten anything.'

The classroom is on two levels. On the ground floor there's a small windowless entrance hall with an umbrella stand and two rows of coat hooks no one ever uses but Miss Robinson; light's provided by a single bulb set into the ceiling like a solitary eye. A vicious, nostril-pinching smell comes from an adjacent boxroom which is crammed with detergents, floor cloths, mops, buckets and brushes, a square porcelain sink, chipped and lustreless after too many scrubbings, and – squat behind a shower curtain – a toilet. A sign above it says FOR SLOPS ONLY, 'slops' being underlined twice.

A short flight of steps leads up to the mezzanine, where the cookery room proper mirrors itself in a window-front that runs the length of the far wall and gives on to the school yard. The four custom-built kitchen areas, all equally sparkling, enclose a space in the centre for tables, chairs and a blackboard on wheels.

When Miss Robinson enters, hidden behind the three latecomers because she's felt it necessary to check through their purchases first, the blackboard's been moved and is just wheezing to a halt near the steps, swinging loosely in its frame like a giant's nodding head. Peals of laughter ring out before she has a chance to see what's been going on: underneath the recipes on the board someone's chalked a puckered-up potato face.

'Watch it, girls, or you'll be staying in again,' Miss Robinson says scratchily and to no one in particular, trying to keep her temper, for the moment at least. Then she points with one of the shopping bags: 'Edith, please, would you mind wiping this off? And put the board back in its right position – if you can manage, that is.' She hasn't meant to say the last few words aloud, hasn't meant to be hurtful, but Edith's unnatural thinness annoys her; it's a waste and an affront, an obscenity really, made all the more poignant by the loose-fitting muslin dress that keeps drooping and caving in on the girl. And *her* talking about boys!

Disgusted, Miss Robinson turns away. She ignores the twitter around her, yet, crossing over to the fridge, becomes aware of walking lopsidedly, as though a piece of mud had got stuck in the tread of her left shoe. Of course she knows it's nothing, the floor's as clean as a new pin, just her imagination playing up again. So she stamps her foot hard twice, and that seems to do the trick. There's silence afterwards. But the class hasn't been taken in by her manoeuvre – they're simply biding their time.

The first period is nutrition theory. As usual, Miss Robinson sits perched on her swivel chair opposite her pupils. They remind her of cutouts pasted on glass, especially now, with the late morning sun pushing in through the line of windows into the room behind them. Pushing in mercilessly. Already, the trees outside have a dark, skewered look and their shadows appear stunted out of all proportion.

Before beginning the lesson, Miss Robinson had swept across the yard with a long, harsh stare that seemed to swirl the litter into a heap out of sight and to bodily lift and straighten up the few schoolchildren who happened to be slouching about. Only the Tinguely Metal Man, the sculpture towering ten feet high in a concrete-slabbed fountain, has remained as he was. Perfectly indifferent to light and shadow and to how or whether they affect his size, he continues balancing his cannon ball, letting it rumble from clawlike hand to clawlike hand, with the easy reassurance of someone who knows how to hold their own. Miss Robinson's gaze keeps returning to him. He's helped her through lessons before.

'So,' Miss Robinson grates, her eyes flitting from table to table, from face to face, 'what are the main constituents of food, then?' She's nicknamed the three sets of girls that make up the cooking teams 'sex', 'meat' and 'brains' – a private joke to jog her memory.

'Chocolate,' Myrtle cries, winking at the others as she smacks her lips rather unashamedly (she is a member of team one, has a sallow face and a sluggish, full-blown body that strains the seams of her dresses).

Miss Robinson merely purses her mouth: 'Anyone?'

Sonja, elbow on table, raises a forefinger: 'Protein, carbo-hydrate, fat.'

Sadly enough, it's the girls of foreign background who are the most promising in this class, Miss Robinson muses as she gives a brisk nod. The local stock is represented either by cuddly little pussycats *à la* Myrtle & Co., groomed and licked and slicked into shape, or a more degenerate strain preoccupied with food (it's impossible not to swivel round towards Edith, half-dead after her little task, and her two friends, Gaby the guzzler, and Kate with her equine features and puritan abhorrence of flesh). Miss Robinson feels an itch of annoyance spreading down her legs.

'Anything else you can think of ? Kalsang?' She looks over at the girl, then away again, but not quickly enough. Because for that one second *there's* Kalsang's brother, his image reflected in his sister's face, his eyes as black and lidless as hers, only more slanted, the cheekbones even higher, bronzier, the lips thin, chiselled almost, though without that disdainful curve ('defiant' might have been an apter description, but Miss Robinson doesn't always choose her words wisely).

'Well?' Miss Robinson tosses her head to shake off the image. A wispy giggle hangs in the air. Her itch is becoming unbearable. She jumps up and begins pacing the room, careful to avoid the advancing shafts of sunlight. The girls are watching her. Miss Robinson never walks, she marches. Like a pair of scissors slamming open and shut. Perhaps she hopes to intimidate them or to make up for the flat-heeled children's shoes she's forced to wear because her feet are too small to fit adult sizes. Now, all at once, she shouts, 'Pull those blinds down, someone! And get out your books!'

It's after eleven, and Miss Robinson has brought herself back under control. She is demonstrating how to prepare the various dishes on today's menu, pretending not to be bothered by the girls' shoulders blocking her view.

'Next comes the ruler,' she says, perhaps a trifle shrilly, and slaps the pink plastic onto the rolled-out puff pastry in front of her, measures, then cuts it with a knife: 'Five-inch squares . . . like this . . . should give you twelve croissants, OK?' Standing on tiptoe for a moment she raises her voice: 'Now for the ham filling – two spoonfuls a square, that's what the recipe's calculated for, no more, no less. Anyway, you don't want to gorge yourselves. Better to . . .'

None of the girls are listening, they've heard it all before. Behind Miss Robinson's back, Gaby's telling Edith not to worry, she'll help her dispose of surplus food no problem – and Kate's share of ham into the bargain. Kate smiles her horsey smile while Edith starts nudging Kalsang, who's staring past Miss Robinson's impeccably bobbed hair at the thick fabric of the blinds, her mouth sneering softly. Kalsang's in one of her dazes, has her brother on her mind, no doubt.

Suddenly Miss Robinson swings round, her eyes fizzy with suspicion. It's a habit of hers, and it does pay off occasionally: this time she's caught Myrtle's hand in the act as it were, picking stray hairs off her best friend's blouse and dropping them casually on the floor; long ropey hairs that coil nastily on the shiny tiles, clearly visible.

'Myrtle, you'll be doing the mopping today.' Miss Robinson's voice dips and dangles dangerously, like a fork ready to pierce. She knows she mustn't lose her grip again and strains every nerve to imagine the Metal Man in his corner, *her* Metal Man – so strong, so utterly imperturbable.

This Wednesday Miss Robinson is eating with Kalsang, Sonja and Angela. She does her best to engage them in conversation, praising the salad dressing, then the artistic shape of their croissants, then re-introducing the topic of proteins, carbohydrates, fats, vitamins and minerals from the most playful angle she can think of: 'They're a bit like friends,' she says with a laugh that bares her teeth, 'or acquaintances, enemies even – to be sought out, ignored or best avoided!'

But the three girls remain silent. They don't like Miss

Robinson. Somehow, she always makes them feel as if they're guests who haven't been invited. She seems to act the part of host – and act it very badly: there's no grace in her performance, no warmth or generosity, only restraint and a tedious obsession with detail. Just like when she tells them to wash up the floor around their kitchen area the instant something gets spilt ('In case you tread in it and smear it all over the classroom'); or when she keeps them in till they've steel-woolled away half their hotplates and vinegar-shined the chromium of their sink and draining-board so insanely it could have been mistaken for an extra-large mirror in a beauty parlour.

Halfway through the meal there's a *tap-tap* at the window in the far corner. It's too faint to be remarkable really, a bee perhaps, hoping to get at the nectar inside the bright red of the blind, or an empty snack packet being blown about – except, of course, that the bees are late this year, and the day windless, as calm and unmoved as the Metal Man's face. Whatever the reason, Miss Robinson, for once, is blissfully unaware, having just bitten into another croissant. But the girls glance at each other and their eyes flicker. Afterwards they talk more loudly and laugh a lot, in a childish, blurting, vulgar way that makes Miss Robinson shrink inside.

Dessert over ('A touch sugary, your *compote*, Angela. Remember that men, especially husbands, don't like things too sweet'), she pushes back her chair with a screech. This is the time when she stands her straightest, her hands lifted for a moment as if to steady an imaginary ball. 'Kalsang, you too! We're in a Christian country here!' Miss Robinson wants the girls to be grateful for the food they cook, nothing more. Ready to have to glare them into submission she is surprised to find there's no problem today: all heads are bent, meek and attentive. 'Mary had a little lamb,' goes through her mind and, folding her hands, she congratulates herself on her teaching skills, then begins:

'For that which we have just eaten may –'

Something has clattered against the windows outside, a whole volley of small stones or nails that will leave the surface pitted with tiny sharp craters no amount of polishing can erase. Miss Robinson is off like a shot, she feels personally attacked, defiled even: to be interrupted in the middle of a prayer!

The girls' lips twitch as they watch her yank up the nearest blind. They know she won't see a soul out there at first, only the dirty emptiness of the yard. They know that as soon as she's flung open the sash to lean forward a group of boys in outsize T-shirts, back-to-front caps and daringly low-slung jeans will come skateboarding into view, gliding past her in single file; and that she'll start yelling at each of them in turn, most likely making futile threats involving the headmaster. And the girls also know that the boys will ignore the shouts and put on a show specially for her, blowing kisses.

Abruptly Miss Robinson jerks away from the window; there was a noise behind her from the boxroom, she's quite sure – the boxroom that should have been *empty*.

'Who's there?' she calls out. No one replies, not a sound. She eyes her class sharply; none of them's missing, none of them moves. None of them looks at her. Kalsang appears to be shuttered in a silent wild world of her own, like a woodcut under glass.

'Answer me!' Miss Robinson rushes towards the steps leading down to the entrance hall, then stops short to listen. Someone's in that room, she's certain, messing about with her cloths and cleaners, her buckets, her mops. Didn't she hear a noise, distinctly hear it, a minute ago? She twists back towards the girls; it's obvious to her they're merely *pretending* not to have noticed, holding their breath all the while.

Miss Robinson is getting very upset. Already she is too upset to focus on her Metal Man. And when she tries to picture Kalsang's brother instead, when she tries and tries and tries, there's nothing but a blank in his place and even Kalsang's face begins to look blurred now.

The only thing Miss Robinson can see clearly as she turns away from her class at last is her own shadow, lengthening towards sunset.

~

Bellaluna

It was a hard job getting Aunt Rachel to change my life; in the end, I had to force her.

I was twelve when we first met, she in her early forties. She'd stopped smoking by then and instead chain-chewed matches, their acid bright heads jabbing carelessly from her lips. She wasn't very well that day, her whole body twisted out of shape because of a slipped disk. But the usual match was in place, smeared with lipstick the colour of dried blood and exposing the moistness of her mouth:

'So your parents sent you, did they? Nothing like youth and beauty to seduce the weak, no?' She rubbed her back for emphasis, grimacing so extravagantly her match snapped and fell to the floor. With another grimace that seemed to indicate pain more than anything she eased herself up from where she'd been slumped against the hall table, to feel around the pockets of her dressing gown. In the gloom behind her I could make out a Christmas tree; white candle wax had guttered over the branches, faintly phosphorescent.

It was Boxing Day; my brother Tom and I were taking her a bottle of port and some Stilton in a purple-glazed jar I'd made at pottery class. Mum and Dad had stayed in the car, down an alley out of sight, engine running – 'for warmth,' they explained, but I knew better. They'd given us detailed instructions beforehand, telling us where to go, what to say and how to smile. And when to leave.

Tom was a sad spectacle, huddled up to me like an extra layer of clothes – he was four years younger and always crawling in on himself – and I realised I'd have to fight for two. Having replaced the match, Aunt Rachel stood biting and chewing till the wood squeaked against her teeth. Her eyes had narrowed to slits and now a glint showed in them, white and pointed as a cat's claw, and as unpredictable. I shot her my deadliest glance, pictured the match blazing up and the rest of her being turned into an explosion, and said quickly, retreating towards the front steps, pulling Tom away with me: 'If you please, we were just passing through and hoped you might . . .'

'"Passing through"!' Aunt Rachel spat out the match and, without taking her eyes off us, pushed the presents we'd given her to the far end of the table, up against the wall. Then she laughed, a grating laugh deep in her throat: 'Hansel and Gretel straying into the clutches of the wicked witch, is it? But don't worry, I won't keep you.'

We'd reached the bottom step when there was a bristly hiss, like she was sweeping the floor after us: 'Now get you back to your parents – before I change my mind!'

The wrought-iron gate shuddered as I yanked it open; a dark bird flew up from somewhere nearby, almost brushing us with its wings. I grabbed Tom's hand and we ran. Her laugh kept chasing us round corners trying to trip us up; garden walls echoed with it, and houses; it boomed and bounced off the cobblestones, twanged through trees, and would have swooped down from the belfry where the clock was just striking the hour – if the car doors hadn't slammed shut behind us that very second.

Mum and Dad were furious. Not because they felt sorry about what had happened to *us*. They didn't. In their view children's minds were like magic pads: a firm tug and shove, and hey presto, not a trace left of blotted memories. They were furious simply because it was obvious Aunt Rachel still hadn't forgiven *them*. But maybe I shouldn't blame Dad too much. He was merely going through the motions, bullied into some sort of supporting act.

'An eye for an eye, that's her all right, cussed as ever.' Mum's nails stabbed into one of the tangerines she'd brought along for the trip, sending the juice spurting down her coat. The air in the car had a sudden sting to it, sweetly pungent and heady.

I'd just sunk back in my seat when Tom started nudging me, all hyper now that we were safe. 'She's got laser eyes,' he cried, 'and she talks with her mouth zipped up, her shoulder's all bent and . . .'

'Rubbish. You shut up and have some of these instead.' Mum tossed us a couple of tangerines which Tom ignored with a fierce whisper, 'It's true. Tara here knows it's true, don't you?'

He turned to me but I never said a thing. I was sucking fruit segments and thinking about Aunt Rachel alone in her house while my hands were crushing and re-crushing bits of peel next to an imaginary candle flame, trying to make it spit.

From then on Aunt Rachel became an obsession with me. I began to eavesdrop, desperate to put things into some kind of perspective, no matter how warped. Aunt Rachel was five years older than Mum and they'd never got on, it seemed, not even as kids. They'd fought over nothing and everything, over all they hated or held dear in the world: sweets, slaps and insect bites, goodnight kisses, cassettes, teachers and, of course, boys. 'Man-mad' Aunt Rachel was called. When she'd left home she'd taken Mum's boyfriend with her — or so they said. Aunt Rachel must have looked pretty good in those days, judging by the handful of photos I'd liberated from an old album (the only ones to have survived intact, in the others her face had been scrawled over with a black felt-tip pen or cut out altogether).

If eavesdropping didn't get me anywhere I'd mention Aunt Rachel's name as though haphazardly, with a bumbling innocence Mum found hard to resist, especially when she was rattled already and in need of a scapegoat — and an audience. Rachel was such a stuck-up fool, she'd say in a high-pitched voice, banging a random lid on a pot or swatting at flies and specks of dust that weren't there; that's why she wouldn't let bygones be bygones, couldn't get it into her thick skull that the twenty years they'd been out of touch were her own bloody fault. How dumb of Rachel to think they'd bother to track her down after she'd run off like that. And the 'clubs' she'd ended up in, for God's sake! Joints they were, nothing more, cheap joints blue with cigar smoke, the lampshades too choked up to shed any light. And anyway – here Mum would pause for an instant, perhaps remove the pot lid with a resounding clash, theatrically – and anyway, hadn't her and Dad done their very best to make amends soon as they'd heard Rachel had retired ('putting her feet up at thirty-nine, if you please') and bought herself that huge house? Wasn't it them had phoned her ever since, once a month like clockwork, to check she was OK? But enough was enough. Mum would be peering at me rather closely by now and I'd be nodding, yes, of course, yes, yes, and hiding my eyes behind strands of long, tangled hair.

Yes, I knew what she meant: ill will, no doubt, and false accusations, spitefulness too, the sort of spitefulness that didn't hesitate to hang up on them in mid-syllable or, worse still, whose deliberate obscenities would come slithering out of the earpiece, wormlike, ready to hook into their flesh and turn it into running sores. But up to that Boxing Day nothing had ever festered, my parents had always humoured Aunt Rachel's fits of temper with an indulgence that seemed a little creepy to me. So when they stopped ringing her I felt kind of relieved, at least they weren't pretending any more – till I realised they had their informers, after all.

More than a year went by. Then, early one hot and sultry August evening, a neighbour slunk through the half-open door, carrying a shopping bag which was dark blue and bulging with the bombshell news she'd brought for Mum.

Had she heard? the woman says, point-blank.

'Heard what?' A nod telling me to beat it, chop chop (only trouble is it doesn't seem to register, so engrossed am I in my homework – and she too impatient to risk an argument).

'Well, about your sister, that's who you keep asking about, isn't it? You'll be surprised. Quite something, really. In fact –'

A quick, sharp intake of breath: 'Oh, get on with it, will you!'

The bag's crackling at the seams, near bursting point: 'Hah, she's upped, Rachel's upped and sold her house! Bought some ramshackle restaurant near the mountains instead, place called Bellaluna. That's what!' Without another word the bag swings round, apparently weightless now and deflated, almost flabby-looking as it passes through a splash of sunlight and is carried out triumphant, leaving havoc behind.

I'd never seen Mum fly into such a rage before, screaming her head off loud enough to rouse the entire village from its late-summer lethargy: 'Damn you, Rachel! Treating us like dirt, you bitch! Underhand, sneaky bitch!'

Dad wasn't home yet so Tom and I rushed round the flat like the dutiful children we were, blindly closing doors, windows and shutters, finally even curtains, cupboards, whatever was ajar. Afterwards we sat in Tom's room, which was furthest from where she was, Tom all hunched up over his electric keyboard, pressing quirky, half-remembered chords endlessly, I with the headphones on and the radio at full blast.

Dad seemed nowhere near as upset as Mum when he got back, just called Aunt Rachel a stupid woman. Didn't she realise she'd always remain an incomer, slightly suspect and looked down upon, in a place like that?

There was an acrid, sour smell in the flat that night, exuding from walls and carpets and clinging to the very fabric of the curtains. An acrid smell, despite the breeze blowing in through the windows which I'd flung open the minute Mum went off to bed, her face screwed up in pain. She'd often said that migraines were like battles or thunderstorms (because these were the worst things Tom and I could imagine), full of crashing, tearing noises and knife-blades of flame right inside one's head. But I didn't feel sorry for her this time. She'd had it coming, I thought. So let her have it.

The next day she was still in her darkened room. And the next. By then, however, I'd made up my mind. If she couldn't face bringing things out in the open, *I* could.

It took me ages to track down 'Bellaluna' on my school map. The name was hardly legible, obscured by a jungle of mossy-brown contours on either side and reduced to 'B. Luna', as though the very existence of the house was threatened or doubtful, somehow. The nearest village was P., and that's where I addressed my letter to.

I started haunting our post office, mornings and afternoons: Please, was there anything for Tara Lee? At last the woman nodded, staring at me ominously from behind the glass partition as she produced a familiar-looking envelope: my own letter, unopened. And all the way home it was like smelling the tangerines again, only more sulphurous, sharp with the piercing sharpness of laughter and loud angry voices. But I wasn't going to be put off that easily, I could be as obstinate as Aunt Rachel – even more so, I told myself.

The second letter, which I posted in town, had a typed address label on it, and a typed sheet inside. It read: '**Top Secret**: Please get in touch with me, Aunt Rachel. I'm waiting. Your niece Tara. PS. Please reply c/o the post office here. I don't want Mum and Dad to find out.'

I waited for three whole weeks, hurried from the post office to school and back to the post office day after day and still nothing happened, nothing except the gradual softening of the clerk's stare and my heart clenching tighter and tighter with the effort to keep a smile on my face. Nothing except Aunt Rachel's stubborn silence, always her silence. The taunt of it. And enough was enough, as Mum would have said.

Next thing I knew I was in a public phone booth, punching out some number I must have got through inquiries, though I couldn't remember making the call. Before I had time to straighten out my thoughts a low scratchy voice drawled, 'Hello –' Then it grew brisker, increasingly shrill: 'Hello? Who's this? Hello?'

The receiver in my hand was rattling against the metal casing of the coin box and I could hear panting, the rapid staccato panting of fear or excitement or maybe both, frenzied and uncontrollable even after the line went dead. A gut reaction, and so spot-on I couldn't help giggling when I'd pulled myself together enough.

I rang her again a few days later, number withheld, during the morning break. Then again, at a different time. And again. No more panting or rattling now, nothing at all, just the receiver lying on its back on some surface nearby, half-strangled by coils of cable, and me watching it. Aunt Rachel must have sussed things pretty quick because she never got irritated, never swore, merely sent the dialling tone down the line while I stood motionless, letting it purr on and on and on till the three-note shriek – my cue to be off.

Of course, once Aunt Rachel knew who was calling, there wasn't much point in continuing. It was like being in a tug of war in which the other party has tied up their end of rope and left. Nothing to be done unless I wanted to fray my end, if not myself, to bits; nothing, anyway, short of cutting the knot –

The following Saturday Mum and Dad were out shopping as usual; Tom had gone round to a friend's. It was one of those October days when the sky's a harassed-looking blusterous blue, and by the time I arrived at P., what with travelling past millions of shivering, shaken trees and telegraph poles and changing trains on draughty platforms, my body too seemed strangely windblown. I got some tea and pizza from a stall outside the station, then set off towards Bellaluna. 'A mile at most,' the vendor had said, wiping his hands on a dirty-white dish cloth, 'you can't miss it.' There was a lump in my stomach – the food, no doubt.

Aunt Rachel's restaurant was open-air: out on the terrace over-looking the river, under a sturdy, retractable tarpaulin she'd had installed to protect her guests against the worst of the weather. Even so the menus, weighted by chunks of silver-speckled local granite, would flap in the wind that came gusting down the gorge a mile upstream, swishing about in the fir-trees and making hot meals and drinks go cold within minutes. On rainy days mist curled and settled under the tables like a litter of wet grey dogs, and the surfaces needed cleaned continually. All this was to become familiar to me in time.

She was alone when I arrived, and seated at one of the tables by the French windows, chewing on the inevitable matchstick and scribbling, frowning into the sun every so often. Around her head she wore a gaudy orange scarf that gave her dress a scorched and shrunken look. A newspaper lay open in front of her. I guessed she must be doing the crossword.

I'd stopped near the steps to the terrace, despite the wind urging me on. I felt ill at ease – it wasn't so much Aunt Rachel's patent unawareness as the alarming flashiness of her scarf. The shiny material seemed to glare in my direction and there was a glow about it, like smouldering heat; at her slightest movement sparks zigzagged across the window-pane behind her and were gone, indecipherable.

Abruptly, everything flared alight: 'Quit that staring, girl, or you'll be turned to stone.' She was a lot taller than I remembered, a lot straighter, more formidable, but the way her laugh caught in her throat hadn't changed.

'Who're you, anyway?' she demanded, bearing down on me.

I said nothing, just kept looking. Kept looking with the wind shuddering around me and those flame colours coming nearer and nearer.

At last she stood still and the scarf became a scarf again. As though some spell had been broken, she, too, suddenly appeared much less intimidating, ordinary almost, and in her very ordinariness bore a strong resemblance to Mum. She was like I imagined Mum could have been – if she hadn't had any children, that was, and perhaps no steady husband either.

With a scrunch Aunt Rachel bit her match in two. 'OK, Tara, you win,' she said. 'But you may find the game's not worth the candle or that it's a cat-and-mouse game really, and *this* only the beginning . . .' Thoughtfully, her eyes never leaving my face, she picked some pulpy bits of wood off her tongue. Then she shrugged, a violent shrug more like a shiver, took me by the arm and led me up to the table where she'd been sitting.

Her habit of speaking in riddles was getting on my nerves. Was she trying to impress me or what? Intimidate, maybe? I felt my old anger stirring; nothing much to lose, I decided, not here or back home – not anywhere.

'I've brought you something,' I said as casually as I could and pulled out the letter that had been returned to me.

Above the wind and the monotonous swoosh of the river a car could be heard grinding to a halt, and Aunt Rachel had already stood up, 'No matter, no matter. You're here, so we'll celebrate, have a drink or two.' She was talking rapidly, mechanically, her eyes flickering past me, down towards the path. Without even a glance at my letter she vanished through the French windows. I was wondering whether to go after her when someone shouted:

'Hey! You the new belladonna of Bellaluna?'

There were two of them. They'd been fishing by the look of it, both wearing wellington boots, jeans and oilskin jackets. Both laughing. The smaller one was quite young, with a wicker basket slung over his shoulder. The other had a beard. I turned away, pretending to be absorbed in the letter in my hand, smoothing the familiar notepaper on the table and starting to read what I knew by heart. But one by one the words seemed to writhe free and lift from the sheet, and on the blankness underneath I fancied I could see my little brother Tom, his clothes looser than ever, running away from me.

The next instant I was back with the men. They were still laughing. They'd unzipped their jackets and sat down further along. Seconds later Aunt Rachel appeared.

'Ah, here she is, *our* belladonna!' exclaimed the man with the beard.

'You're early,' was all she said. She was carrying a trayful of bottles and glasses, and clamped under her elbow was a French loaf. As she passed me I noticed a fresh match in the corner of her mouth, an extra long one this time. The scarf was tied round her waist now, burning her dress in half.

'Couldn't wait, love,' the young man grinned, 'to show you these.' He unfastened the basket, held it open for her to see: 'They're for you.'

Aunt Rachel had put down her tray and was leaning over him, her back to me.

'Big enough?' the other man asked. Someone chuckled raggedly and there were sounds of slapping and the smell of crushed bread.

Afterwards Aunt Rachel began to set out the glasses. 'Why don't you join us, Tara?' Her voice was rasping rough, like the side of a matchbox.

I looked away, across the empty tables towards the river and beyond; the wind seemed to be getting fiercer, making the tree tops bend and swell, bend and swell into the sky, wiping it clean, a pale ashy blue in which the birds scattered like cinder.

~

The Ladies' Man

Neil stood brushing her hair with slow, measured downstrokes, having a giggle to himself. The standard lamp was on, and *there* were the reflections in the window: a big shadow swaying over something thin and withered, propped up against a tangle of gleams. Those metal bits belonged to a pram, a kingsize pram, and the figure inside was an old, old baby girl whose hair clung to her skull in flat, moonwhite stillness. Every evening it was the same, the shadow reaching into the stillness, trying to brush it alive. Most nights he succeeded, and his mother's hair would spring up at him suddenly, like a cat-o'-nine-tails, making him flinch at a pain he couldn't forget, as if she was bursting into his room even now, to see why he wasn't ready –

When her hair remained lank and lifeless he'd feel just as bad: punished because he hadn't been punished. But being able to giggle helped; whatever happened, it helped keep him sane. And she didn't seem to mind; on the contrary, her eyes were shut so firmly she looked like she'd been asleep for a hundred years. Some princess *she* was! He laughed out loud and speeded up the brushing.

~

Old Mrs Thistle had woken a short while ago because her spine was hurting and she felt itchy in the extreme, worse than a flea-ridden dog, in fact. Though to oblige her son she had pulled herself together and remained quite motionless, in comatose discomfort, as it were.

A little less brushing and it would have been such a pleasure to leave her hair in his capable hands. She had always loved her plaits: thick and glossy and reaching all the way down to her hips when she was a young girl; later, during the first few years as a school-teacher, coiled intricately round her head, not a pin amiss or a single hair; and finally — with Neil something of a household name in town — shorter, silvered and intensely private, a luxury reserved for her own room, at night.

Now that he was spluttering with laughter she had a pretext for stirring at last, thank God. 'Please, Neil,' she said, yawning to delay the moment when she would have to raise her eyes and meet his disappointment, 'would you please stop the brushing and get on with the plaiting? I'm dreadfully —' It was then she noticed the bruises on his face. Had he forgotten to take his medicine again? Ever since that first fit she had done her best to remind him, warn him . . . Surely she could not be held responsible? She pursed her lips, '— dreadfully sorry.' Waiting for his voice she wondered whether he had heard her at all. He was gazing out into the darkness, brush in hand: so far away. If only her health had not let her down, then the two of them would still be keeping house together, or rather she would be keeping house for him, and he need not have given up the salon and moved into the nursing home with her. He was not even a pensioner yet, let alone an invalid . . . But the manageress here had promised to keep him on his toes as a live-in hairdresser-cum-barber for the old folks, those were her very words. Besides, who would be running wild at *his* age, fifty-five last spring, and risking a good reputation? She smiled indulgently and bowed her head.

~

So that's how it was: princesses didn't wait to be kissed awake any more, instead they turned into hags right away. Or wicked witches. For they never meant what they said. Like this one mumbling 'sorry' after she'd made it dead plain that all *she* felt was tiredness. So that was that.

Except that *he* was feeling squeezed inside out, guts and everything; and his laughter had shrivelled into silence. In the window he caught sight of the shadow-man with his shadow-brush held high, like an unlit torch. Just a few seconds more and her hair would have been floating. A few damn seconds. He glanced down and, running straight and pink towards the tip of her nose, her centre parting exclaimed back at him. Shrilly, accusingly. So she must have registered the bruises after all – and filed them under his 'fits', the myth that kept her safe. He'd better offer some sort of reply right away or she'd be on about those tablets again.

'Well, mother,' he said as quietly as possible, patting her shoulder, 'why don't you go back to sleep and leave me to it? If I rearrange your pillows . . . there now, you'll be comfortable enough, won't you?'

She made no answer; perhaps she'd dozed off already. He craned over to look her in the face: no, he couldn't be certain, not yet, not while her eyelids had that mothy flutter about them. He'd wait and do some plaiting to lullaby her. The rest of the brushing could come later; as long as he knew it would come, the waiting didn't matter.

She was a little girl now and her flaxen hair needed attended to by an adult. By someone who knew their job. Using a comb he parted it down to the nape of her neck with never a graze, never a single graze, then started on the first plait, flexing the strands into curves slowly and gently, almost lovingly, pampering her. Of course he knew she was an old hag really, a wicked witch sometimes, and always his mother – he wasn't daft, or blind. But he loved to pretend her bed was a pram and she his baby, his baby princess. Things had a symmetry like that, a beginning and an end; and the end never truly did end but began all over again, over and over. Like the sweep of a woman's hair as she bends forwards forming a perfect circle perfectly cut from left to right and right to left, only you can't tell which is which, ever.

He'd been famous for the precision of his cuts; even long straight hair he'd managed to style to perfection. And now, well . . . He shrugged and, for a few seconds, stared at the plait in his hand,

then he shrugged once more, picked up a piece of silk wool —
only the softest material was good enough for his darling princess —
and looped it round.

Perhaps she *had* fallen asleep. It was about time, high time. He
held his breath, leant nearer, but her eyelids trembled, the veins on
them stood out in twitches of blue. Blue-blooded, indeed! He
grimaced. Yes, he *had* given up his salon because of her, because
he'd been led to believe the nursing home could do with a
proper hairstylist. Not a shampooer of bald patches, for
chrissakes, or a shaver and trimmer of beards, nostrils even. Just to
think of such closeness, such intimacy, the intimacy of skin
touching skin, his skin on theirs, the skin of other men — It made
him want to grab the brush and . . .

*No! No, don't! Imagine her hair instead, her hair that afternoon so
many years ago, streaming wildly as she came tearing into your room
without knocking, remember? Then in one long heavy plait crudely
knotted at the end, much longer than now, much heavier, and inflicting real
pain, flailing sears of pain right across your face, the palms of your
outstretched hands; and your fly still open. Later that first frothing at
your mouth, and your eyes hard and blind as stone. Yes, you do
remember this, don't you? Already your hands are unclenching, slowly,
slowly the muscles in your fingers are slackening, one, two, three and
there you are, see, fiddling with nothing more than the strands of hair that
are going to make up the other plait. Good boy. Keep at it.*

~

Mrs Thistle lay there resting. She had let Neil adjust her pillows
without a word of protest so he would realise she was not
bearing him a grudge. To allow him his due, he had done it
rather well: her itch had vanished, and the pain in her spine was
easing off now. But she could not help wondering what on
earth was going on in that head of his. He looked more than a
little sheepish, especially with those newly permed curls . . .

And then all the brushing as soon as he thought she had nodded off; the way he started to giggle, giggling himself mindless – or that was what it sounded like, at any rate. Though at present there was not a whisper to be heard, only the driest of dry rustles and the feel of his hands as he plaited her hair for the night. Time and again she had marvelled at how soft his fingers were, how very light his touch, a discreet caress almost.

No surprise he had been such a favourite with the ladies in his salon, had, indeed, already become a favourite here, too. Even as a schoolboy he had won women's hearts: 'nature's wizard' they called him when he tended their gardens to earn some pocket money – no one could clip bushes and trees with greater precision, plant flowers in more exquisite patterns, in circles and squares and triangles so the beds appeared to be embroidered by rainbows. Naturally enough, therefore, she had expected him to qualify as a gardener, highly skilled and esteemed, a gentleman's gardener.

On the other hand, being a successful hairdresser had given him so many opportunities. God knows he could have taken his pick of nice, bright women. And him the eligible bachelor *par excellence*! She had done her best to reassure him, often and often. 'Your epilepsy is no problem, my dear,' she would begin, 'don't you worry about it. I have asked the doctor, and he says in your case there is absolutely no danger of passing it on to the next generation . . .' Always at this point Neil would interrupt, saying wasn't he lucky to have *her*, such a wonderful housekeeper and homemaker, he couldn't be luckier.

Of course, that was before they had decided – independently, it must be stressed; she never failed to remind Neil of his independence – to leave Greenwood Crescent and had settled here, over two months ago, he in what they called a self-catering unit, she three floors up in a private room. She had been taken down to his place in a wheelchair a few times, duly admiring the dozens of bonsai and faultlessly *coiffured* wigs he had salvaged from the salon. But, on the whole, it was no doubt easier for him to visit her.

She became aware of a familiar tightening about her scalp, a clean, prickly sensation which normally meant he had finished the plaiting. Normally; not this time, however. She had lived too long to be fooled and knew that he had barely even begun with plait number two: her dear son was daydreaming – though she rather wished he would not clutch her hair so. Well, she would be patient for a little longer. Had endurance not always been her *forte*?

She gritted her teeth.

~

Once this plait was finished and his mother safely asleep, he'd have to untie the silk, untwist the strands and continue the brushing. Brushing and brushing to keep himself from harm –

But they needn't have turned against him last night. They'd been his pals from when he'd moved here, Mike and Brian and Tom and John. 'Hey, Neil, old man,' they'd say, 'how about getting in an extra round?' and they'd pause, grinning, maybe slap him on the back. He'd never refused – how could he? – they had families to provide for, after all.

He straightened up; that was the second plait dealt with, ready for her inspection if she was still awake. Next came the magic gel. Two drops should do the trick, two drops to soothe and seal her split ends. His fingers flicking as if they were weaving a spell.

So hard to resist, especially Mike with his neat moustache and that full head of hair all sleek and wavy and bluey-black. They'd talk football, jobs, women. Mainly women. He'd have to answer endless questions about 'the birds' at the salon. The slightest hesitation and they'd start nudging him, between nudges throwing in a few jokes about pubic hair. 'Don't be silly,' he'd reply, 'I always did my best for any lady, whether teeny-bopper or granny.' By now the others would be licking their lips like animals on the prowl. And if he insisted he hadn't really gone for his assistants, that, quite frankly, those blouses falling open every time they as much as snapped their scissors shut had rather irritated him, they'd all be wolf-whistling and he'd be forced to make up stupid stories. So he took it they were friends.

And he'd never touched any of them. Never. Never dared tap them on the shoulder even. Somebody must have jostled him last night – that was why his hand had got caught against Mike's jeans. He'd tried to pull it away, tried desperately, but it seemed jammed there until Mike started to yell at him. Then everybody was yelling and punching and kicking and he was on the floor. Thank Christ he'd learnt how to fake one of those fits or they'd never have stopped.

Neil passed an arm over his face and winced.

~

She was waiting for him to finish and get that gel business over with. Surely, singeing would be a much more effective cure for those 'splits' he kept going on about, pretty unpleasant, she understood, but at least a once-and-for-all, like shock therapy. Why he would not listen to her, Mrs Thistle had no idea. Tentatively, she put up a hand, a mere reflex to check whether the plaits were fine; yes, each twisted as smoothly as a rope's end, and each precisely above her ears: she could not have done it any better herself.

Smiling, she let her hand fall back on the covers and opened her eyes. Then shut them again instantly. Keeping them shut against what she had glimpsed, much too close for comfort: his bruises and beyond them . . . what a look! – blurred and unfocused, yet intent too. Who needed a husband, with a son like this? The question had been her rallying cry since Neil's earliest childhood. And to see him exhausted to the bone after a long day's work around the elderly and senile, let alone an epileptic fit . . .

Well, she for her part would not trouble him any further; and without much ado, half-asleep already, she slid her head down the pillow in a graceful little nod that left the two plaits spread out on either side – a gesture of praise, perhaps, or gratitude.

~

Small wonder he preferred the ladies; they were so much easier to handle, they and their vanity. They never seemed to lose that, not unless they went off their –

Neil jolted upright, blinked. Behind him the door had opened, cutting a square of corridor light into the reflections in the window. Just like in one of those Advent calendars there was a picture underneath here, too. Only he couldn't bring himself to look more closely . . . couldn't take his eyes off it either, or turn and bow, ever the accomplished gentleman, couldn't do anything at all until a woman's voice said, 'Sorry, Mr Thistle. I'll come back later,' and the square narrowed, narrowed down into a faint *click*. He shook himself, rubbing his elbows, numb from being pressed against the metal frame of the bed, and allowed himself a smile at this time-honoured privilege of the private patient, the paying guest. But then, inch by inch, mulishly, his eyes pulled him back to where, a minute ago, the window had opened out into another window. Already he could feel a low-down sickness welling up, up, up . . .

Because you've known all along, haven't you, what that picture really showed. You're not blind, or daft. So forget about princesses, forget all about that hocus-pocus. Just clamp your teeth together. Tight, yes. Tighter still –

Like when you were a boy pruning back shrubs and trees, and the twigs would poke you in the eyes, would wiggle and wag at you with crooked fingers, making V-signs and thumbing their noses. And you lopping away at them feverishly, sore and dizzy from shearing round and round the same tree, the same shrub, and they getting thinner and thinner, but never quite perfectly shaped –

See, on the pillow? So fat and knotted. Lying in wait.

Not a noise now, you don't want to wake her. Quick. They're in the drawer here, right next to you. Yes, they're nice and sharp.

Ready? Quick now. Before she moves her head.

Remember. Remember that afternoon.

Remember?

~

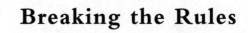

Breaking the Rules

This time it would be all right. Faces and number-plates were like cyphers: once decoded, everything fell into place. Neatly. She'd learnt how to do it, and no mistake. Despite her parents' warnings, their threats and tears. Now she'd left school she was her own mistress; other people's paranoia didn't matter any longer.

Of course, if she'd wanted to, she could have made the train home to Anders. She could have run and the summer heat would have left her all limp and sticky. The leather seats, scarred with roughly stitched-up crosses, would have pressed into her bum and thighs like open sores.

And then the kids. Schoolkids. Always blocking the aisles and bragging about their petty deceptions, their cleverness. Such cheats. *She* knew all about that sort of thing. About inside soles sweaty with mathematical probabilities. Stocking tops guarding the laws of economics or the secret of the earthworm's sex-life. She knew about fresh paper hankies which, held close to your face for that irrepressible sneeze, would suggest rosewater and the delicate ramifications – past, present and future – of *aimer* in different moods.

It was mid-afternoon, and the streets quite empty. The lunchtime downpour had left a string of puddles along the kerb that winked at her every time she as much as moved her head. In the nearest, streaks of petrol were slinking out as colours of the rainbow. Pretty enough. Pity about the sky though, its vastness all soiled into ragged patches of blue and wispy white. With the end of a stick she ripped open the surface, stabbed at the water till she made the mirror go black.

Some of the muck had splashed over her sandals. For a moment she wriggled her toes in its soft ooziness, then bent down with a crumpled-up train ticket and started to rub. Scraping the skin red and sore. Still scraping when she heard it – a low growl which suddenly exploded into a roar as the motorbike rounded the corner of Station Avenue. She straightened up, flicked back her hair. The lights further down were red so there was no need to put her thumb out just yet: she'd let the bike come to a stop and flash a smile towards the visor.

Well done. And the driver was right on cue too with his left hand raised lazily to acknowledge her. Fumbling with the strap under his chin in shy awkwardness. So, should she accept? His vehicle looked great, chrome-plated and everything, like one of those choppers in *Easy Rider*. Not that she'd have much chance of getting a decent conversation going. But it would be different. Exciting. With the air sucking round their bodies, and her legs as smooth and cool as marble –

Shit. The lights had changed and there he was, turning left and not even bothering to indicate, only the smear of his teeth trailing behind. What a sham. Playing hide and seek, was he? Not with her though, no, thanks. Past the bank, the supermarket, past the school, disappearing behind the police station, gathering speed now, racing uphill towards the cemetery, not giving a damn whether he blasted the flowers on the graves. Thought himself king of the road, did he? Well, she could hardly see him any more. Fading along the gloom of trees and tall old houses into a mere fly's buzz. King of the road? Sod him!

How rigid she'd become. Achingly tense. If she was at the office now, she'd make a dash for the toilet and, with her back against the wall, fall to frigging herself. Out here, all she could do was ravage her nails. To hell with the unchipped coral pink. The little finger first.

Those two women were taking ages to waddle by. Craning their necks with their beaks almost touching. What did they mean, parking their shopping bags in front of the photographer's window? None of *their* pictures on show, that was for sure. Unless they were watching her reflection, of course . . . Huh, she'd give them the time of their lives. Slowly, slowly she began moving her hands over her breasts and down to her hips, writhing and spitting bits of nail into the puddle where the rainbow had re-formed.

Nothing more soothing than being a little rude sometimes. The two hags had beaten it. All she wanted to do now was close her eyes, keep them closed, and let the tugs of pain at her fingertips merge with the sunlight burning under her lids.

Several cars slowed to a *purr-purr*, windows were wound down. She shut her eyes even tighter – she wasn't that desperate. The squeaking glass was enough to give her the shudders, never mind the creepy chat-up lines: 'Hey darling, let's go for a ride!' or 'Want to earn some money, honey?'

And that automatic swish a second ago? Brisk and smooth, a businessman by the sound of it, and he seemed quite genuine: 'Can I help you, young lady? Are you OK?'

Such clinging concern, though. Boring her stiff already. She yawned with her mouth wide open. Like that toddler asleep on the bus the other day. His mother had been pestering him, prodding and jabbing and hissing his name. He'd simply pushed her away, his lip all curled. How weary he'd looked, how indifferent; not a single glance towards the bunch of kids with their bird cage or the crazy old woman across the aisle who'd been moaning on about being 'sick of shadows'. He, at least, had learnt self-control. Lucky little devil.

'You hitching?' A deep voice.

'Yeah –' She blinked, 'Thanks for stopping.' This one was wearing cowboy boots, and his eyes were different colours: greenish-grey on the nearside, light brown on the other. A posh blue Audi. But what about the number-plate? She couldn't see it. The car had pulled up no more than a metre away – and she hadn't bloody noticed. She must be stricter with herself. Readiness was all: 'Where're you going?' Perhaps he'd lost one of his contact lenses. Shouldn't she check his number-plate, decode it? Her hands were clammy.

'Anders – not very far, I'm afraid. I can drop you off in the centre if you like.' He smiled at her.

He was chatty all right. A good omen. She'd better ignore his eyes, forget about the number-plate. 'Suits me fine.' She smiled back, wiping her hands on her dress.

Diagonally behind the car, the wooden walls of the station had weathered to the sheen of raw silk. The next train was due in less than a quarter-hour.

He called himself Tony. Said he was a commercial artist with his own small firm. That he liked computer games and country music. Had taught himself guitar. Loved preparing food for guests, played squash, and sometimes had a pint or two. She'd met his type before.

Why didn't he want to tell her about his friends? His family? So pigheaded. Always chipping away with, 'And you, what do you do?'

Eventually, she found herself talking about the clothing company. About phoning and faxing and feeding her Mac. About dealing with complaints – worn elastics, fraying selvages, faults in the dye – child's play really, once you knew your customers. Today had been sales statistics on men's underwear:

'Bet you prefer ordinary Ys? No fancy pants for you, eh?' She burst into giggles.

'Can you drive?'

She shrugged, 'Sort of, I'm still a learner.'

'Enjoy it?'

'Oh, yes –' Wait a minute, hadn't his tone become sharper, teacherly almost?

'Get much practice?'

This was definitely turning into an interrogation. But she wasn't at school any more. Not her. She could see the river now, glittering brokenly through a line of black poplars. Her teeth clenched, she kept staring straight ahead till her eyes felt strained and raw and the road was rushing in on her.

'So, would you like a go then?'

Was he trying to make fun of her? He didn't even know her. Once at the wheel, of course, she wouldn't be able to fight back, and he might do all kinds of things: slide his hands inside her dress, touch her breasts, or maybe start to touch himself. Still . . .

'I'm not sure –' She crossed her legs.

'No strings attached, if that's what you're worried about.' A pathetic attempt at coughing, then: 'I've full insurance, you know.'

She thought he'd darted a glance at her out of the corner of his greenish-grey eye, and for an instant she studied him curiously. His gaze fixed on the road, he never batted an eyelid, and the fringes on his cowboy boots hung motionless.

They'd reached the bridge. Against the water's glare the poplars looked bleached and ineffectual. His generosity was a bit too good to be true. A cover-up, probably. Well, so what? Why should she feel under any obligation? It was *his* suggestion, after all. And if he did become overfriendly, she'd threaten an accident. Nothing like blackmail.

'As long as you don't mind arriving home late. I'm not very fast . . .'

He brought the car to a halt on the grass verge.

He was on about his job again. She only half-listened, heard him mention labels and logos. Computer-aided graphics. On-screen colour simulation – whatever *that* meant. Must be married to his work, poor bugger. But what was this he was saying? About maybe showing her round his firm? No reason for him to do so, really. Anyway, she ought to concentrate on her driving; they were getting closer to the vineyards upriver and the road was much narrower here, with some nasty bends.

He drizzled on.

A zigzag, and she hadn't used the brakes once. The secret was changing gear at precisely the right moment. And power-steering. She felt great. Everything was under control: the road, the car, the afternoon. Tony.

All of a sudden he said to go right. The winery? What for? She didn't want – No –

'Hey, I explained a minute ago I'd have to hand in a couple of designs for bottle labels up there. Nice hairpins, too.'

Some challenge! The lane squirmed through the vines like a caterpillar drunk on the smells of earth and stone and dry wood. Tony remained silent all the way to the estate. As he was reaching for his briefcase on the back seat she heard him gabble the old cliché about taking things easy.

'Yes,' she said. 'And you.'

She woke with a start: Tony was tapping at the window. Decent enough, considering. Because he could have sneaked in and – She gave him a quick smile.

'Had a good nap? Christ, what a furnace!' He recoiled in mock-horror then, briefcase in one hand, door in the other, swung them to and fro rapidly a few times before climbing in beside her.

She bowed: 'Becoming one of my fans, are you?'

They both laughed, and she switched on the ignition as if the car was hers. It seemed natural to ask how he'd got on.

'Fine. The manager was rather taken with my ideas. Promised me some complimentary bottles of this year's harvest.' He paused. 'Actually, I might let you have one – in return for your taxi services.'

What the hell was he talking about? This was the beginning of July, and the grapes not even ripe yet. Without turning her head she mumbled how very nice.

'Well? Enjoy hitching?' A second's hesitation as he shifted in his seat. 'Pretty dangerous for a girl on her own, I imagine.'

Was this *his* chat-up line? She changed down, indicated and rejoined the traffic on the river road. Neat job, but he hadn't noticed a thing. Not one single word of praise. Taking her for granted already. Not enough that she was chauffeuring him round the countryside, oh no, monsieur evidently liked to be entertained as well. So that was why he let her drive his car: he wanted to be trusted, wanted to worm his way into her good graces.

Hadn't he moved again just now? Manoeuvring his body up against hers, was he? She jerked away. Never mind the swerve, the opposite lane wasn't busy. He was yawning, but she'd heard him gasp all right. That should teach him. She chuckled and went faster, overtaking a 2CV decorated with giant ladybirds.

He was leaning towards her, his brown eye very dark suddenly, 'Slow down, please. No need to break the speed limit.'

She let the needle drop, 'I was merely testing the car.' A farmhouse passed in a blur, its windows ablaze with geraniums or begonias. 'Not bad, really.'

The road was becoming less wriggly, cutting across a patchwork of cornfields, woods, and orchards with dun cattle behind wire fences. Why didn't he speak? Worse than that little boy she'd seen on the bus. Had he gone deaf, or dumb, perhaps? His shoulders stooped, his face was blank.

The air had grown hotter. White heat like liquid glass. Soon it would be crystallising round her. Smothering her. She should say something. Get him loosened up. A story. She'd tell him a story. Her throat made a rasping noise:

'Once upon a time a man offered a girl a lift. He had a smart number-plate, was bright and cheery and began cracking jokes that made the girl shake with laughter. Gradually, however, he changed his tune . . .'

How she hated roadworks – and the lights had just turned red. She glanced over at Tony: still in his stuffed-dummy mode; what was the matter with him? She gripped the wheel harder. When green came on, she accelerated with a screech, stalling the car.

Someone hooted.

'You left it in third gear.' Tony's voice.

'I know,' she said. 'Of course I bloody know,' she repeated a little louder. 'It's your fault. Expecting me to make all the conversation –' Sweat was trickling down her forehead, eating into her eyes. No air-conditioning. Christ, what a crappy car! 'You do the talking from now on. Tell me about yourself. The truth, this time. No more job-and-hobby shit!' Her hair was such a mess, all damp and sticky. She wiped her hand on the upholstery, then pulled the gear lever straight down. The engine revved.

'If you'd stop at the next lay-by, I think I'll –'

Second instead of fourth. 'Something's wrong with your fucking gearbox!' There were dribbles of sweat running down the sides of her nose, searing her mouth.

'Well, it's never caused *me* any problems. Anyway, you've done enough driving for today, let's just –'

Smartarse. '"Never caused *me* any problems"! Huh! So what *are* your problems, sunny boy, tell me?' The taste of salt on her tongue, sickening . . .

'In here!' His arms were flailing.

Even if her head was near to bursting, she played it real cool. Yet another sloping bend and hardly a skid. She was doing fine. That bastard on his bike couldn't have zoomed through it any faster.

'Stop it, OK? Stop the car!'

'What? You don't want to talk, is that it? First have me do all the work, then ditch me?' She'd show him. She wouldn't let go; he'd have to prise back her fingers, every single one of them. Gritting her teeth, she pulled the wheel closer – closer still. Yes, she'd show him all right. But the wheel seemed so slippery all of a sudden; and why was it beginning to twist and turn in her hands? Why was it making those faces at her, such ugly, leering faces? She couldn't bear –

When she recovered herself, the car had stopped, her door was ajar and the seatbelt unfastened – no harm done. Tony was sitting by the roadside, his head on his knees. What a wimp. She slid the keys from the ignition and got out, feeling much better already. But he didn't even look up, simply sat there, reeking of self-pity. Without a word she went across, jangled the keys over him.

'Please –' he began and raised his eyes. They were the same at last, almost black.

She smiled, 'You just don't understand, do you?' A few steps towards the car, a playful little wave, then she drew back her arm.

The keys caught the sun before they fell somewhere in the high grass. 'Safe journey home!' Another wave. No more worries about his number-plate now, or the colour of his eyes. She grinned and kept walking. There'd be another car soon.

~

In Here

'No, this is Thursday, not Monday. Thursday – got it?' I smile at her, my teeth clenched in neighbourly restraint, while my elbow slowly, stealthily, juggles the door into her toad-stare. Just as the latch clicks shut I repeat in a loud, firm voice, 'Thursday! OK?'

But almost immediately there's another of those *ratatat-tats*. She's become so persistent recently, a bloody nuisance, to tell the truth, her knocks sounding more and more hollow every day, more and more bony. Not much longer now and they'll be leaving splinters behind, tiny sharp bits of knuckle stuck in the panelling of my door, and a faint gleam of ivory, or metal keenness . . .

I don't bother to open up this time, simply rattle the inside flap of the letter-box hard and furious, wrenching it off almost before shouting through: 'Thursday, Thursday, THURSSSS–!' The sibilant's got caught in my throat somehow and I'm hissing at her, can't help it really, hissing and screeching like an animal in the dark. At last I hear her shuffling back across the passage and, after what seems hours frayed and trodden out of shape, the thud of wood on wood as she closes her door. Then nothing. I lift my head. My eyelid's begun to twitch again.

Of course, it's not Thursday; that's just one of my private jokes. Gives her something to puzzle over. Because the bins are out, piled sky-high bang under her nose, their knotted tops gusting up like crows' wings, only less synchronised, more violent, swishing and flapping and flinging themselves against the window-pane to haunt her behind curtains as filthy as cobwebs – and, off her head or not, she must know the bins are collected on *Wednesdays*.

I manage not to slam the hall door and return to what's left of my breakfast – cornflakes soggier than loo paper, the coffee afloat with a greyish slick of skin. My eyelid's still jerking away, and when I pour myself a fresh cup half the milk spills over. All in all not exactly a great start to the day – but then, if it wasn't for my sense of humour, I'd have moved weeks ago.

Though in a strange sort of way I'm quite at home here, too. Maybe Steve was right, maybe I *have* ended up a masochist. I can't even seem to get rid of his voice, goddammit.

'Now that's a case in point,' I seem to hear him say. He sounds pleased, vindicated. And all at once I feel his arms pressing down on me, ropes of muscle tautly slung across my chest, but I mustn't panic, not while he's stroking my head with his fingernails and breathing into my face, breathing in such frenzied concentration there's a snail-track of sweat along his upper lip. Perfectly still I wait for the words I know by heart, and again I cringe as he mutters them, lopsidedly, between one grin and another:

'Yeah Rita, you're so fucking virginal people just want to draw blood . . . Want to scratch that ivory pallor of yours, claw and rip it till the colour shows . . . Like a kid rips a rag doll to see what makes it smile . . . or whimper . . .'

Red-hot tweezers plucking at my eyelid, zigzags of pain. I can't hold out much longer, I have to open my mouth, wide, yes – Next moment the twitch has gone, stopped in mid-spasm. I blink a few times and wait, just to be sure. It's then I become aware of the silence around me, the space. There's no one else here.

Lots of things I need to get used to, or the light will always be too bright, the wind in too much of a rush, catching me unawares. I kick back my chair and set to clearing the table, briskly, in a series of pounces that remind me of the tortoiseshell cat out in the garden – my neighbour's cat – and how it will attack those gooey cornflakes. Slinking from behind the old wash house it'll creep up the blue-green path laid by the shadow of the industrial chimney halfway across the lawn, pausing only at its outermost edge, where the sun hits the ground, pausing, then suddenly stiffening because *I* am there – *still* there, when all it expected was a bowl on a ledge and a closed sash – its whole body rigid now except for the tip of its tail, curled a little and flicking the grass like a miniature scythe. We stare at each other, stand and stare, the cat as stubborn as its owner, while I begin to shiver in the morning chill.

But that was yesterday, of course. Today's different. So, instead of repeating the same boring games over and over, I put the bowl on the ledge, pull the sash back down and snib the window. 'Have fun!' I cry, banging the kitchen door shut with a laugh.

Things are on the mend for a change, and it's not nine yet; plenty of time to tackle a couple of boxes before Geoff picks them up after lunch. Two boxes, that's five hundred envelopes – five quids' worth of addressing, junking, sealing and sore hands. Or: five quids' worth of not-having-to-stay-with-Steve. So what's the choice? And if the old dimbo across the passage feels like cracking her knuckles, who cares? She certainly won't provoke me, not after last week. A whole load of leaflets dumped right over her head, and it didn't even scare her off; took me ages to flatten them again.

Now for today's goodies, let's see . . . Holiday brochures: 'Sun, Sea and Fun for less than the cost of your annual cable TV. Plus: Win our Competition and travel around the world for 365 days – via satellite!' The usual crap. I get the mailing list out, unscrew my complimentary fountain-pen – cobalt blue ink for the personal touch – and start on the envelopes, working through the alphabet bottom-up because the sequence seems less familiar that way, faster, with the letters pushing ahead in leaps and jumps. Quite a few men this time, but what names! 'Hugo Zouzou', poor sod – XXX on the flap to cheer him up, there; 'Archibald Yellowstone' . . . 'William S. Willis' . . . 'S.' for ? I'll make it 'Sean' and he'd better be thankful; the 'Steves' go in a separate pile: the empties.

Where on earth are those binmen? Such a wind's sprung up in the last hour it's driving the bags outside crazy. They're heaving and scraping the ground, beating their wings more frantically than ever, and they've got that shifty look, like they're about to take off – 'Wendy', not '*Windy* Mackintosh', stupid! The rest's simple:

'21 Main Street, Bilsten' – to hell with the post code. Anyway, that's it, no more addresses for now or they'll be luring me on again, on and on till I'm left in some dead-end street with all the houses bricked up and no people, just the glare of the sun. I'll do the brochures instead, folding them's nice and straightforward: align the corners, put a finger on beach boy's smile, then two quick flicks of the wrist. And there's his girlfriend, garlanded with scarlet flowers and holding up a drink to toast their holidays; she hasn't realised she's been shoved to the back, of course, and that she's smiling at a headless man. She won't ever realise, not after ten or thirty or a hundred brochures. Not after a million.

Steve would never have let me toast him like this. He'd either have taken hold of the glass, casually crushing some of the blossoms against my collarbone, saying, why didn't I lie down now in that deck chair (comfortable enough, wasn't it?), lie down properly, without posing; or he'd have walked away, towards the shade of the nearest coconut trees maybe, or up to the poolside bar, though certainly no further because he'd want to keep an eye on me, like some damn bodyguard.

Just to prove him wrong I went with another man once. He had thick curly hair worn in a ponytail, his stomach was soft and there was something Mediterranean about him, something warm, irrational. So I went with him into the house where he was squatting and together we climbed this long winding stair past rooms from which laughter rang out and the sounds of eating, higher and higher past silent doors he'd push open to show me 'the sights': an old grand-piano without lid, its strings fingered by streetlights, heaps of smashed-up furniture – 'See those bits? Used to be chairs nobody ever sat in, real pains in the backside!' – and walls stripped and scoured to bare plaster, down even to the ribcage pattern of the laths; the house was going to be renovated any day now, he said. The top floor felt damp because the roof had been pulled off in parts, but through the thick plastic sheeting you could make out the moon, smudgier perhaps, and more crumpled-looking, yet the moon all right. In the end he never showed me his room. And I never asked.

Well, that's half a box finished with, neatly stacked and folded – one hundred and twenty-five brochures for as many suckers. And their number's growing . . . Steve would have a fit if he knew what I was doing. Always on about my 'youth and beauty', my 'freshness', and how I ought to preserve them, shouldn't let myself be 'ravaged' by work:

'Spoils your complexion, Rita, and remember, blotchy-faced, bleary-eyed fucks are a dime a dozen . . .'

Still, the few hours he allowed me in his shop every morning didn't do me any harm, did they? Far less than all the bloody time I spent hanging around at home, waiting, mouth fallen open and generally in such a stupor I couldn't tell what was outside or inside any more, like I was leaking into things – magazines and sofa cushions, the surrounding air, the walls, empty space even – and they into me. What's so hard about selling jewellery, after all? The customers? Or earrings that won't unclasp, tangled-up chains, dead watch-batteries? Steve could never find the slightest damage when he'd sit scrutinising me at midday – eyepiece poking into my face like a huge glass tentacle, and that fierce 150-watt lamp drawn up close on the workbench. Couldn't leave me in peace one second. 'Just checking,' he'd say, and how did I feel, whether this or that, what was I thinking and when would I, why hadn't I –?

The doorbell; who the hell . . . ? I almost knock over a pile of brochures before I realise it's that shoddy mirror again, above the mantel, rattling and buzzing and tinkling itself into such a blur of dizziness it'll go blind next. And then I hear the tell-tale rumble: the dustcart's on its way at last. No danger now of the binbags' flight and of wasteful clouds, white with the shine of reflections, white and shivering . . . Time for a break, anyway.

I go up to the window and, lo and behold, there's my good old neighbour out in the street, waving her nylon housecoat like she's trying to flag down the binmen. One of them's started to speak to her, over his shoulder, while lugging along an old mattress. But she doesn't seem to be listening, just keeps gesticulating, slapping that ghastly housecoat of hers at his hands even, real mad stuff this, her jaws loose enough to fall off. She won't be staying around much longer, that's for sure. The guy looks pretty pissed off, and I don't blame him. All of a sudden he drops the mattress, grabs her by the arm and – shit! he's seen me, because he's pointed in my direction and she's nodding, won't stop nodding now, and here they come, Christ, straight towards the house.

Moments later I fling open my door. I know what I'm going to say.

Instead she's being pushed at me.

'No, please . . .'

He's blown his gum into a giant bubble that explodes inches from my face. I take a step back, putting a hand up to my eyes. Too late though, the twitch's like a live wire already, and he's out-tricked me, pushing her in further still so I have to move aside if I want to avoid that vacant dangling grin.

'Don't you let Gran run amok again. Or I'll tell the authorities.'

She's mumbling something and I say, 'Thursday, Thursday,' automatically.

'Fucking bedlam in here!' He taps his forehead, chewing and sneering with savage teeth, then turns to go.

She's more than half inside, he nearly out the front, and I'm trapped in the middle. 'You don't understand, hey you!' I charge after him. 'I'm not her keeper, she's not –'

The door's crashed shut.

At night I lie awake, thinking about Steve. He was like a stone someone had dropped into me and I was a well. I'd learnt to tense myself so there was no flesh to bruise, only brick-hardness; you could hear him as he fell, a rush of air, echoing hollowly. But somehow, despite the falling, falling he never reached the water.

Not once. The well must have been very deep. Even when we made love I could hear him and felt the hollowness, neverendingness of the fall.

~

Getting Rid of the Gods

She could hardly make out the shadow of the model plane on the reservoir's surface. The sky, sullen and pinched-looking, wouldn't let the sun poke its sticky fingers through the clouds, and the water had turned as blind as the eyes of the gods she'd found back at the house. At least she could hear the steady *whirr* somewhere above the trees. So much for Uncle and those whisperings last night.

Why on earth had she bothered to follow Paul and Mark up here? Cousins or not, she could have stayed behind improving her croquet instead, the garden all hers for one long morning with Uncle painting away in the studio. Also, it would have been easier to get rid of the gods. Much easier. To hide them now she'd have to wander off into the forest, which would set Mark snooping after her. Unless, of course, she pretended to need a pee –

Nobody was going to spoil her plans, she'd see to that.

It's her first day at Uncle's, and she's passing through the dungeon. That's how it feels, anyway; the hall's so cold and gloomy. The light trickling down from the upper landing has an exhausted look, as if it's haunted by the jungle of leaves that grip the banister and claw their way over the walls and ceiling.

But what's this? She stops dead. The foliage near the staircase rustles and sways, and there, looming out of the half-shadows, are several dark figures. Their eyes seem to curdle as she looks at them and their lips twist. The gods! She can feel her flesh creep. If you ignore them, they punish you. Is that what Mark meant to tell her? She shudders, breathes in deeply. Bows. Maybe too hastily. Because all at once a flame springs through the leaves with a squeal and a thump. Are the gods so quick to take offence? She starts to run, peeps back just before the corner:

Ginger, the cat, is chasing a mouse across the stone floor.
As soon as they'd parked their bicycles where the path ended,
Paul had gone off on his own. He'd have to concentrate, he said,
particularly the first time. They didn't want this to be a disaster, did
they? He was holding the model plane under his arm, almost
embarrassed, and for a second she could see the fear in his eyes.
Then Paul smiled, suddenly tall and five years older again, 'You can
help me tomorrow before you leave, OK, Moira?' She'd nodded,
managing to look bright and happy and not in the least
concerned, and had walked off without another glance at the
carrier bag she was leaving behind, wedged between the saddle and
the mudguard of her bike. The carrier bag with her anorak on top.
There'd be masses of time to sort *that* out.

Now Mark was fishing a few yards away. He didn't pay her
any attention: he was already in secondary school and knew
everything. But she was getting clammier and twitchier by the
minute; sitting at the muddy edge of a reservoir in a forest was a
real pain. Her dress had become a sweaty mess, her back hurt
where a tree trunk pressed into it, and her legs were grimy with
dirt and that stuff Uncle had forced on her.

'For a healthy tan in a jiffy,' he'd said and held out an oily tin.
His skin looked a bit too much like a slowworm's. She tried to be
polite, oh no, thanks, she was fine the way she – Grabbing her by
the arm, Uncle had begun to rub the grease on her face, 'If you
don't know what's good for you, I'll have to teach you. Just like the
boys.' What was he doing? She tried to wrench herself free, then
went limp almost instantly. No need to put up a struggle. She
was going to stop him being threatening. And there'd be no time
for him to get back at her: Mum and Dad were coming to take her
home tomorrow.

Paul was so much nicer. He was the older brother she'd never
have, and he still let her see his room. His room! It was more like
a cockpit because pasted around the window on the far wall was
a huge poster of a pilot and co-pilot behind hundreds of

switches, levers, buttons and little screens. She must suggest swapping the picture of the jumbo jet above the snowy mountains for one of hers, maybe the wild horses or the monkey dressed in a sailor's suit.

Paul was cool. Everybody said he took after his 'poor' mother. But who could imagine Auntie Jane with a crew cut and bouncing along in Doc Martens, jeans full of holes, and a 'Star Trek' T-shirt? Nobody'd ever explained what had happened to Auntie Jane. The only thing she could remember was an autumn day and being fetched from kindergarten to a chapel where a man read out a story Auntie had written for all of them about an island and waves and the sand disappearing under her feet. The chapel stood in a woodland park, and scattered among the big old trees were gravestones which looked very white and lonely in the rain. That's when she'd first sensed Auntie had done something wrong.

But if Paul was supposed to take after her, then, surely, Auntie Jane couldn't have been so *very* bad? Was it possible that sometimes goodness was a sin? And wrongdoing a blessing in disguise? The carrier bag – what would Mum and Dad say once they found out?

She was getting really itchy with all those pine needles and insects. Some healthy tan! The mosquitoes left smears of wings, broken bodies and blood at her fingertips. And they kept coming. They were stinging her ears with their little propellers, they were making her sneeze, they were falling apart on her tongue –

She jumped up, spitting; enough was enough. She stamped on the ground, trampled it underfoot; she wouldn't sit and wait any longer. Shaking her head now; she couldn't care less. Shaking it so fiercely she felt her lips wobble into numbness and her mind go blank.

She froze, her left leg in mid-air, and nearly fell over. Mark was looking at her; he must have said something. He was smirking.

'What?' she panted.

His grin broadened: 'You got mad cow disease or something?' He made as if to punch the air but even she could tell he was anxious not to knock over his fishing rod.

'Girls –' Mark wrinkled his nose, turned away and spat into the water. From where his spittle had hit the surface, rings began rippling towards her.

She's hurrying up the stairs behind him and her suitcase. In the dim light the red leather gleams a dirty brown. Then she stumbles over a loose fold in the carpet and, clutching the banister, touches spiders' legs on polished wood. Mark has heard her shriek and laughs before she's time to realise it's only ivy, trained around the handrail and the poles supporting it. He's already reached the landing, throws open the nearest door. As she climbs the last few steps he blurts out:

'And, Moira, mind the gods. They don't like girls. Especially girls who rush about poking their noses into everything.' He dumps the suitcase on the threshold, and it topples over with a thud. Is he testing her? Or simply teasing? He can't mean it. When she gives him a quick smile he glares at her. What's wrong now?

'The revenge of the gods is sweet.' His face has hardened into a mask of stained wood, lids seared around eyeballs, mouth and nostrils wide with darkness. She can't move; something's twisting inside her and trying to uncoil. That phrase: she's heard someone say it before, but it's all a tangle of blurred memories, far away. She shivers in the cold shadows, clasps her hands and waits. There's nothing else to do.

Abruptly, the sun returns, swirling motes of dust through the skylight and touching her with its warmth. She starts towards the stairs.

'So?' he sneers, coming closer.

'I'm not nosey or anything, if that's what you think.' She speaks rapidly, to get it over with. 'Let's be friends and please don't talk to me like that again, it's so unpleasant.'

'Unpleasant?' he pushes her aside, pounds downstairs with his head flung back, roaring like a jungle beast.

She'd stolen up to where Mark sat perched on a heap of stones, humming to himself. A gentle kick, just to attract his notice.

He dropped the fishing rod.

'Caught anything yet?' Her voice sounded shrill and loud. No time to think about the dark forms gliding away towards the centre of the reservoir, Mark swung round much sharper than expected and dodging him didn't help because he grabbed her by the hair instead, pulling and tearing and making her eyes water. All of a sudden he let go and, with a disgusted face, started picking long blonde strands off his fingers.

'Bastard!' she shouted back, yards away already. She was running fast now, her breath rattling in her chest like a toy in a wooden box. She touched her head to feel for bald patches, clots of blood. It wasn't her fault she was a girl, was it? 'Asshole,' she gasped. She'd never used the word before: 'Asshole.' She rolled her tongue round and round it as if it was a bad tooth.

She didn't give a toss where she was going. And the forest couldn't be that big anyway. She'd come out of it sooner or later, in time for Mum and Dad, in time for the beginning of term when she'd be in primary six. For a moment she imagined making her bed on moss and dry leaves. Birdsong would wake her at dawn or maybe the wet nose of a fox. She might even have a camp fire for company and to keep the mosquitoes away. But there were no matches, no food. And wild berries could be pretty sour –

When she slowed down to look over her shoulder, the reservoir had disappeared. And so had the path. All she could see were the long shoots of some shrubs and weeds swaying back into place. Her scalp throbbed, taut and raw, and she felt a stitch coming on.

What if she got lost, though? She didn't have any breadcrumbs, or white pebbles. And the carrier bag was miles away. She could have smashed the gods into bits right here and now, leaving a 'paper chase' for Uncle. Even if he *had* brought them all the way from Africa, he mustn't ever get them back. Not after that row last night. Not after she'd seen how he used them to frighten her cousins. Had Uncle scared Auntie, too?

Thank God she wasn't *his* daughter. Or she'd never have dared to unhook the nasties from the wall.

Without the slightest gust of wind the creepers start to scrape against the plasterwork in the early morning stillness, and the black figures seem to squirm and wriggle, almost slipping through her fingers. She grips them tighter. This isn't her home; they can't harm *her*. She puts them in the carrier bag one by one, hiding them under her anorak. Their spell has to be broken. Once and for all. They're evil.

A splash of light came soaking through the trees; the sun was out at last. She closed her eyes and bent over to ease her stitch, letting her fingertips rest on the ground.

Uncle, of course, would blame Paul. He'd yell at him or speak in that low, knife-blade tone, telling him he was a coward and no son of his. That he wanted them back. Up on the wall as before. Or there'd be trouble. Big trouble. Then he'd storm off into the garden and cut some grass in a cold fury or rip out half a bed of carrots for the rabbits he kept behind the house. Or he'd go and paint another of those pictures getting his beard all splattered, and at mealtime Sue, the housekeeper, would slap the food on his plate as if she was rapping his knuckles.

No sooner are Mum and Dad out of the house than Uncle starts showing her round his studio in the basement. He's going to have an exhibition soon. The first since Auntie Jane died. The biggest ever.

'Nowadays,' he says, 'my recipe for success is abstraction. It's so much more expressive, don't you think?' He points to a large canvas splotched different shades of brown, white, grey and black like the fur of an animal – except for the puddles of red in between.

All his paintings are the same: they're all furs, and each fur is seamed with red. She smiles and nods, just to be on the safe side, wondering whether the students at the art college always agree with him.

Then Uncle lets her do a picture of her own – on the door of the rusty fridge in which he keeps his paints: a pink sunset with a rabbit family playing about in a field of poppies, cornflowers and buttercups. 'A *real* picture,' she says after she's finished, and he asks her would she like to see the '*real* Rabbit Heaven'? She claps her hands, all excited.

But the room he's led her to isn't even blue, and the floor looks damp and stained. No grass, no stars, no sun. Clothes-lines and long cruel hooks in the ceiling, a washing machine, a sink with a black plastic hose . . . She's so near to tears her eyes are burning.

Uncle's saying something about Auntie; that she'd been squeamish and stubborn, taking their dirty clothes to the launderette rather than washing them in there. At last he puts out the light: 'Still, Jane chose to come here in the end. To minimise the mess she was going to make, no doubt.'

The blood had rushed to her head and she was all dizzy when she straightened up. But the stitch had gone. She'd better get a move on; forests weren't endless, were they?

How hungry she felt suddenly. Ravenous. With no chance of some half-forgotten, half-melted piece of chocolate in the pockets of her dress, only the crispbread, dry as cardboard, she'd smuggled from her plate at breakfast so she wouldn't have to eat it. At least Sue was going to lay out some food and drink for their return. Sue was great, despite her clicky false teeth, the grooves in her fingernails. And she fed the cat behind Uncle's back: 'Can't let the poor thing die while your uncle airs his daft theories, can we?' Because it was Uncle's boast to tickle Ginger with his beard until he spat at him, saying that here was a prime example of the survival of the fittest: 'Milk and mice this one lives on. See how healthy he looks.'

She was starving, and crispbread was better than nothing. The crumbs tasted of sweat and grease and old fluff. As she was forcing them down, something grabbed her by the ankles, seared her skin. She gasped, swallowed the wrong way and almost doubled over. Brambles, she was knee-deep in brambles. And they weren't even ripe yet.

By the time she'd made it to the pile of logs next to an oak-tree her legs were bleeding. Some of the scratches were really deep, the flesh underneath grey and spongy-looking. Crying, she smeared spittle over them. She cried a little more; nobody could see her here, least of all Mark.

The oak-tree wrapped her in the dusty twilight of its leaves, and again she heard the knocks as the mallets hit the balls.

It's her second evening. Uncle's disappeared into the studio, Paul must be doing his homework. She is 'cousin cock-eyed' and fighting back her tears. She can't guide her ball through the hoops. She can't guide it at all. Mark's finished his first round and stands watching her. The ball rolls into the gooseberry bush, and he sniggers; into the fishpond, and he jeers at 'wets'; finally it goes down the slope towards the road, but she doesn't wait –

She wiped her face. She was much better at croquet now, and somewhere just out of reach Paul's plane was circling and circling. Tomorrow they'd fly it together. He had promised. Until recently they'd hardly spoken – she was too shy and he always doing something or other. So when he asked her, quite out of the blue, did she want to help him with a paint-and-varnish job, she'd been pretty flabbergasted.

Like a giant bird it sprawls on the bed, freshly sandpapered and rubbed down with white spirit. While they're painting its wings and tail Paul switches on the radio beside him. But she can't understand a thing, it's so crackly; and the few phrases she does pick up don't make sense – until Paul explains about alphabet codewords. Then he holds out a hand, 'Welcome on board, Mike–Oscar–India–Romeo–Alfa,' and she knows they're friends.

'Imagine travelling through India with two men in an Alfa Romeo,' she cries, adding triumphantly, 'or wearing a uniform – a pilot's flying jacket, for example – and having a daughter called Alfa in Lima!' Because 'Paul' becomes Papa–Alfa–Uniform–Lima, she's worked it out herself.

Paul looks pleased. He pauses for a minute or two, his brush dripping red paint on the carpet, and she quickly shoves a newspaper over the stain. 'I suppose,' he says, and his voice is almost as crackly as the radio, 'making your own model plane and navigating it on remote control *is* the first step towards becoming a pilot.'

She slid off the logs. Her skin stretched tight where the blood and spittle had dried round the scratches, and for a moment she felt faint. The forest was getting bigger and bigger. Perhaps she'd better go back now. Back to her cousins. She'd make sure to sneak past Mark and up to the bikes for the carrier bag, then bury those horrid wooden men somewhere nearby. Not before she'd spat on each of them in turn, of course. They were demons, not gods. Later, at Uncle's, she'd cram the bag deep down into the bin and rinse her anorak under the hot tap. No trace must remain. Not a smell.

And if she didn't find her way back to the reservoir? Would she tell Paul about her plans? Because Paul was bound to come looking for her at some point. His voice would reach out through the trees, and the fear she'd glimpsed in his eyes would be gone.

The fear she'd felt so keenly herself last night.

Dinner over, Paul smiles at her and announces he's going to test-fly his model plane tomorrow, and that with a bit of luck he might take part in the flying competition next month. Uncle doesn't say a word, just stares at them one after the other, a stare that makes her cringe, it's so hard and dark, as if he's trying to lock them all up in it. What's going on? She glances over at Paul, at Mark, but their eyes are glued to their empty plates. Not a noise anywhere, even the fridge has gone silent, and Ginger's slunk away from his milk by the door, his tail a rigid curve. Then Uncle plucks a glass jar off the draining-board and, holding it up, starts to march round the table.

'Like that time Jane and I were having breakfast in here and we heard a high-pitched drone in the air. A drone that wouldn't go away. That got louder and deeper . . .' he's begun to shout and she can feel his breath push out in sharp gusts, 'deeper and louder till it drowned out everything else!'

Now the jar's nose-diving, and all they can do is duck their heads. She wants him to stop. Stop. Stop. She wants to get up and leave. But already the attacks are growing fiercer, the voice a hot blast:

'A bomber tumbling out of the sky, spiralling towards the house, trailing smoke . . .' Uncle keeps stomping round the table, rocking their chairs with his free hand. She's shrunk into her seat. What's up with him? His eyes are staring, his mouth is a black hole. Mark sits very still and Paul's nearly in tears.

'Then the explosion in a field nearby, then the windows –'

Glass shatters in the sink. A chair crashes to the floor. Paul screams. And Uncle's standing over him, panting:

'Just as cowardly as your mother used to be. Hiding under the table when she should have trusted the gods in the first place.'

She'd almost fallen over a root. The sooner she reached the reservoir the better. Mark might be frying fish, though a hundred to one he wouldn't give *her* any.

How chill the air had become; the sun seemed to have vanished altogether. She was in a dell overarched by high old trees, the slope closer to her a wilderness of nettles, thorny shrubs and bushes, with birds flitting in and out noiselessly, like ghosts.

Well, *she* wasn't scared. She brought her foot down hard. Again. And again. No use; the fallen pine needles muffled every sound. She clapped her hands. Once. Twice. More and faster, like the rattle of a machine gun. Suddenly twigs rained down on her. She threw up her arms to cover her head. A *creak*, a s*wish* and there, flapping above her, was a heavy grey bird.

A heron. Just a heron.

But herons stayed near water.

The slope was strewn with boulders, some of them pushing against tree trunks, others embedded in thick patches of starry white flowers that came up to her knees and gave off a pungent smell. It was damp here, and the mosquitoes a real pest. Waving a hand in front of her, she continued to make her way up.

She's in the bathroom after dinner when she hears Paul and Uncle. Paul's speaking rapidly. He's saying Uncle likes hurting other people's feelings, that he's fond of destroying things; then something about shooting rabbits and feet washed in blood. But why should anybody want to wash their feet in blood? Surely, they'd have to wash them again afterwards?

Uncle's getting very angry. He tells Paul to shut up. That Paul's totally mistaken. And ungrateful. He's been both father and mother to his children. Rearing rabbits to keep them alive. Teaching them right from wrong –

There's a loud snort, and Uncle hisses that Paul is proud and pride is sinful. That Paul would have to pay for it.

What's Uncle on about now? She can feel her heart beating faster.

'Just remember the gods . . .' The words are like a slap in the face.

'Bollocks! To hell with you and your damned black bogymen!'

A door slams, and Uncle murmurs, 'Well, well, we'll see.' His words seem to be echoing all through the house and, once she dares slip out, even the creepers in the hall are whispering them.

But she isn't afraid any more. She knows what she has to do.

The ground was levelling out, and she stood still: no sign of the heron. Some hundred yards ahead, though, sunlight was streaming in among the trees, colouring the branches and leaves a hazy yellow. A clearing. She might make out the reservoir from there, or at least the model plane.

Twenty more yards. Where was that smoke coming from? Already slowing down. And those voices? That sound of wood splintering? Holding her breath, motionless now. Two people crouching in front of a fire at the far side. A crew cut, jeans – Paul! And Mark! Another snap, followed by a loud cheer. What were they doing? They couldn't be frying things. Not with the flames so –

Paul's stood up, her anorak and an empty carrier bag in his hands.

She wonders briefly about the model plane. She can't see it anywhere. But maybe that's not important now.

~

Easy Does It

If only the girl hadn't glanced up. It wasn't his fault. Ratcliffe was annoyed and pleased in a perverse sort of way that made him flush all over. He'd done his best to pass through the carriage unchallenged; he'd walked softly so the soles of his shoes wouldn't give a creak even, cradling the duffel bag with its unexpected sharp edges, his eyes safe behind shades, fixed on the black lettering across the door at the other end. But then he'd sensed a movement near him, had smelt the perfume that clung to it − And all of a sudden it was too much. Too late. Because he'd seen her face now, half-tilted towards him for the merest instant, sunlit, shiny and so *real*, before she turned away again to stare out of the window − and how the hell was he supposed to resist?

He'd intended to sit in the carriage up front, right next to the engine, with no other passengers to crowd and tire out his mind, yet here he was already lowering his heels, forced to a halt by sheer curiosity, the stupid professional curiosity that seemed to dog him wherever he went these days; and the harder he tried to throw it off the scent the sneakier, the more insidious its sniffing − though, usually, the more precious the 'find' . . .

'This seat taken?' For a moment Ratcliffe wondered if his voice had sounded quite casual enough. He'd been thinking of his shades, imagining how they would frame the girl's twin reflections, like sepia miniatures, in gold; and how there wouldn't be any optical distortion except where *he* wanted it, in the curve of her forehead, perhaps, or along those shoulders twisted away from him.

The girl had hesitated and, after looking quickly, for no apparent reason, towards an elderly nun in the section opposite, shrugged without another glance at him, then shook her hair out till it made a screen. Well, well, he'd soon get *that* sorted. He smiled, dumped his bag on the seat by the window and sat down. The nun was absorbed in a paperback − rather a worldly paperback at that, judging by the skull and crossbones on the cover and the greedily furtive way she had of flattening the pages.

How on earth could he have persuaded himself that today was going to be darkroom drudgery, pure and simple? 'A holiday for you,' he'd promised his eyes, less than an hour ago, in front of the bathroom mirror. They'd had that raw look again, a reddish glare, and whenever this happened he knew he had to be careful. A 'holiday' – what a laugh!

He let his head loll against the seat and half-shut his eyes, pretending to sink into the early morning torpor of the average commuter, but really aiming to watch the girl more unobtrusively through the gap beneath his shades – not that she'd notice, of course: she hadn't moved as much as a muscle since cramping herself into that corner. Now and again, when the train went past patches of woodland, he'd catch her face fleetingly, side-on, reflected in the window-pane. He liked what he saw and pictured the rest: flecks in her irises, blue veins showing at her temples, the teeth small and milky. Such a perfect sitter she'd make, even in the most uncomfortable positions . . . Ratcliffe checked his watch, then stretched out his legs. Half an hour still to go, and no more stops; she couldn't run away from him now. He decided to give her a bit longer, a chance to 'uncramp', as it were, before he'd start to loosen her up himself. Meanwhile, just for the fun of it, he'd play a little guessing game; the girl's hair, her hands, clothes and shoes were all the clues he needed. The sun was warm on his neck as he bent forward, ever so cautiously, to get a close-up view, trying to bring out all kinds of things, like what she did and where she came from, her social standing, age and health, her dreams, or fears . . .

He hadn't got beyond her hands, a little strong-boned for his taste, though shapely and well-kept – the only eyesore a heavy gold ring in the form of a snake, but that could be sloughed off easily enough – when the nun across the aisle speeded matters up very conveniently. She'd put her book away and begun to eat an apple. A hard, almost penitential apple by the sound of it, because every time she took a bite its flesh creaked, then chunked off with a *crack*, jerking the girl out of her corner at last. He removed his shades:

'Hi.' He grinned at her and, indicating the nun who was chewing and gaping into space, said in a lower, confiding tone, 'By their fruits ye shall know them.'

The girl smiled uncertainly. Probably didn't get the joke, Ratcliffe thought. Aloud he said, 'I love that smile, it suits you.'

He looked her full in the face, for the second time, and again was struck by its *realness*. He could barely stop himself from reaching out to touch it: gently at first, then he'd clamp it with his fingers, hard, so the shine of her skin would rub off leaving chafes, and harder, till –

Abruptly, the girl tossed her head. Her smile had vanished. In its place was a hostile, slate-grey stare whose directness took him by surprise. He realised there wasn't a second to lose; beating about the bush wouldn't do, he had to knock her right out of it.

'Sulking?' he asked, 'Don't you like compliments?'

She sat on silently, motionless and unblinking, though he could have sworn her stare had grown darker. A moment later her hands were up and she was pushing at her hair, smoothing it away from her brow. Her eyes had fastened on his bag.

He was tempted to say, 'Guess what I've got in there for you,' just to tease her, but instead coughed politely and introduced himself: 'Call me John. So glad to see you're in a better mood.' He laughed.

'Never you mind fuck all!' Her voice had a cold glitter in it.

A tough little bitch, and no mistake. Ratcliffe tut-tutted in pretend disgust, pointedly turning his head towards the nun to test her reaction. But she never even looked up. Quiet as a church mouse now that she'd finished her apple, toying with the core, letting it slide from palm to palm rhythmically, prayer-fashion. The toothmarks stood out in sharp relief, glistened, and in a flash he remembered the skull and crossbones on the cover of her book. No, that woman wasn't praying, couldn't be – more likely to be weighing up the sins of others. He nodded to himself, managed not to chuckle as, with a finger-flick back at the girl, he addressed the nun:

'So, what are this one's chances of going to heaven then?' He must have caught her red-handed because she flinched, blushing an ugly, violent crimson as if she'd been slapped, and dropped the apple core. It rolled away in fits and starts – a dirty grin that belonged to no one.

There was a pause, long and hot and full of stickiness. While it lasted, Ratcliffe tried to gauge the shadow of his face in the far window. The girl's reflection seemed to have vanished, but when he looked more closely he saw it had blended with the nun's in a weird sort of double exposure. The nun had regained her poise and lost her colour, her skin pale again, matt, almost translucent. She was gazing at him with the calmness of a spirit at rest.

'Heaven's no laughing matter, young man.' She set to rearranging her coif, tugging and pressing till her forehead creased in a permanent frown.

Her assumed air of superiority riled him; even if her fingernails were cleaner than his and her conscience more purified, that didn't give her the right ... And anyway, he was damn sure she was sweating like hell under that black habit of hers. 'Like hell, just like hell,' he muttered to himself.

'Pardon?' The nun was frowning all over now.

He couldn't help a quick snort of amusement before offering an apology: 'A private joke, you see.'

There was no reply. Instead he heard the girl's voice, icier than ever: 'Go play with yourself! Piss off!'

For answer Ratcliffe merely patted his bag; better to let her cool off a little. He noticed a half-smile on the nun's face and her eyes seemed to glint at him with something very like *Schadenfreude*; then she was leaning towards the girl, flapping out a winglike arm and saying: 'Easy does it, easy.'

He smiled back as smoothly as he could, which was no more than skin-deep, to reconcile her and gloss over the disappointment he felt at the girl's behaviour: she'd come into the open rather too soon and a touch too willingly, was practically flaunting herself. He put his shades back on, jamming them up against his brows so his eyes wouldn't show, then bowed his head in a sleek, discreet gesture of defeat or regret or whatever, chiefly for the sake of appearances, and let his imagination run away with him:

The girl would be on the model stand, drenched in the sunlight of his most sophisticated lamps: her skin's damp from their heat or maybe from the anger clutching her, genuine, stark raving anger that makes her snarl down at him and spit and bare her teeth, not quite so milky in reality or so small either, and blind passion's exactly what he wants, yes, there's nothing like this head, these feet and stripped fingers ready to stab, slap, kick and butt him – if it wasn't for certain preventive measures, invisible, of course, and loose enough to allow her room for manoeuvring without any danger of hurting herself or jeopardising the *realness* of the pictures. Next thing she's broken free and is lashing out at him –

And he was back on the train, jumping like a jack-in-the-box because the stupid nun was prodding him, asking was he all right, he'd been panting dreadfully a minute ago . . . Christ Almighty! Such an eager look she had suddenly, the proverbial Good Samaritan now that she thought he'd got his 'just deserts'. Ratcliffe waited a while then answered, deadpan:

'Nothing wrong, thank you. I must have nodded off and had a bad dream or two, what with our charming little misunderstanding and the young lady here shouting abuse so early in the day.'

As expected, the nun had gradually stiffened back into her seat; by the time he'd finished she was nothing but a pillar of reproach, immobile against the changing landscape outside.

The silhouettes of factories, warehouses and office buildings were beginning to push the sky out of sight. Already, the train was cutting through the rose bushes, sunflowers and vegetables strangling the edge of the city. The girl was glaring straight ahead, unseeing, obviously determined to stick it out for the remaining few minutes. He must be quick, Ratcliffe told himself, and salvage what was still salvageable. He snapped his fingers in front of her, very softly, like the swish and rustle of someone going through a pile of old photographs. *Snap-snap*, a bit louder, more insistent, and her eyes would come swivelling round. He prepared for his lowest laugh, then stopped himself.

She'd stood up and so had the nun, and now they were homing in, the nun's habit fluttering, alive, its folds and corners making sharp little pouncing movements, the girl's hair about to swoop as they hovered above him and blocked out the light, breathing stale air into his face, looking him up and down, up and down.

'Hey,' he said with a thin smile, 'what's wrong? No sense of humour?' He felt for his bag, hugged it close.

They just stared, hawk-eyed and pitiless. Then they were gone. Words floated back towards him like so much spoilt film, and as useless. Words about some girl. Some guy – or was it *same* guy? A train last week. Girls, guys, trains: who cared? Everybody was bustling now, feet were shuffling and papers being folded away, people getting into coats, clogging up the aisle; impossible to make out anything any more, impossible to go after anyone, quite, quite impossible.

The train's come to a halt. There's a soreness in his eyes and a frantic kind of roving he can't control. They seem to bulge and dilate in an attempt to hold the confusion of shapes, patterns, colours, contrasts that keep sliding past. Every so often pain flares across them, vicious like the striking of a match. It's hard not to wince and easiest to shut them for a while: for as long as it takes him to recover his usual self.

Super Vanilla

Mary has always loved calendars. Or so she's been telling me for the past half-hour. Ever since she met me off the airport train. After twenty years of being apart, with oceans between us and cyclones, snowstorms and avalanches, earthquakes even – the only thing my only sister can think of as we kiss hello is *calendars*.

'Tina, dearest,' she cried, her face crinkling up as if with genuine emotion, 'at last! At last you'll be able to see my collection.'

I must have looked pretty puzzled because she repeated, almost pleadingly this time (though she should know there's no need for pleading with me, her own flesh and blood): 'My collection – surely you remember, Tina? Calendars were my first love, way back in primary.'

Her eyes were on me, enormous and still, like specimens under a magnifying glass. I hesitated. I was quite certain Mary had never been bothered about calendars before; those mountain calendars she'd kept sending me Christmas after Christmas – well, they didn't really count, did they? So I just smiled and gave her a quick nod, then turned away, lifting my head towards the Alps to breathe in, once again, their hateful snow-coldness. Poor little sister, I thought, cranky old Mary, you've lived alone here too long.

Later, when Mary shows me round the house – as if I hadn't spent my entire childhood in the place! – I understand why she was so keen to forewarn me: the rooms are chock-a-block with the blasted things. Calendars climb up and down walls. They straddle tilting mirrors, radiator racks. They swing from doors in poster-size (Narrow-Gauge Railways, Castles of Europe, Marine Life – that sort of thing), scraping and scrabbling along the wood like hands in the dark. Others crouch on tables, chests of drawers, shelves and window-sills, ready to pounce, at the sheerest brush of a sleeve, and spill their landscapes, flowers or *Art Nouveau* nymphettes all over the floor. My room – or rather 'the guest room' as it's now called – is no exception: there's a stack of specially selected copies right next to the bed, 'to help while away the sleepless hours,' in my sister's immortal words.

Naturally, I feigned interest at first, went straight up to some of the more striking displays, Volcanoes in Action one of them, Movie Stunts another, and Mary, with that big happy grin of hers, began sifting through the pages. In the end I was forced to ask her to stop. So many, many days we'd have together, I said as gently as I could (on no account would I want to hurt my dear sister's feelings). But I'd simply have to sit down now, please. How about one of those delicious mangoes I'd brought her, fresh from my garden in paradise? 'And don't forget the vanilla tea on the hall chair,' I added. 'It's the very best there is: Super Vanilla.'

My cup's empty again and Mary's talking about the delights of sharing her home with calendars: 'They keep me company, such lively, varied company. It's like taking the world inside and letting go, time after time: once a month, a week, day by day or, if you happen to own one of those fancy American a.m.-and-p.m. calendars, every twelve hours even! Just imagine, Tina. Much better than TV! Or choosy customers!' Her laugh sounds oddly familiar, though wrong somehow, displaced . . .

'Cicadas,' I murmur to myself, and smile.

Mary doesn't appear to have heard. 'I'm on a rather good pension, you know,' she continues, pushing her tea away untasted, 'and whatever meat I buy I get at cost. Despite early retirement.' There's a note of quiet triumph in her voice suddenly, as if she's been waiting to tell me all along, and for a moment I feel my fingers stiffen, feel them want to grab hold of her, to squeeze and shake some sense into her – like that time she announced to Father and me, completely out of nowhere, that she was going to be apprenticed to the local butcher. Meek little Mary a butcher's apprentice! Mary who'd always been so obliging, so anxious to please.

From where I sit near the window the Alps look like scrag ends, veined and tinged a dirty, pinkish grey by the late afternoon sun.

'Yes, yes,' Mary insists, though I have no idea why. Perhaps it's my eyes, perhaps they flickered once too often and she noticed. My cup is still empty.

Alone in my room at last I decide to lie down a little before supper. It's dark outside, a thick, stony darkness so different from the quicksilver nights on the island I've come to call home. Even the stars seem smaller here, colder, with hardly a twinkle left, as if they'd shrunk into themselves, freezing over shiver by shiver. Suppressing a shudder, I'm bending down to take off my shoes when my forehead hits the stack of calendars by the bed. And all at once things happen. Are happening: my feet in the pile which isn't a pile any more, only so much paper getting crushed, the scrunch of spiral bindings and someone's voice saying, over and over again: 'Now you know. Now you know. Now you know what you've come for . . .'

Then I realise it's my own voice, all hoarse and stifled-sounding after a mere few hours back in the valley, back in the house. When I was little, I used to think the countryside around us had been made by a giant trying to grind up a glacier under his heel. Grinding right into the bowels of the earth where the light doesn't reach. That's why the people here have always had this dank shadow feel about them. But Mary's going to be saved. I'll save her. I'll save her like I saved myself all those years ago.

Yes, she'll return home to my island with me. We'll get on fine, the two of us; she'll take to her new life like a lizard to the sun. No more burrowing, no more hibernating through winters that have gone on too long already; just the heat rustle of leaves, rainbow birds darting their colours in and out of the sky, and dreams punctured by the *chat-chat*-chatterings of the geckos. And there'll be plenty of people to meet – Ananda for one, spraying and wiping and dancing her broom across the bungalow, singing her Creole phrases; then Ramesh, the snack-bar noodle king with his huge wooden forks and a face like Neptune; and Sushilla, of course, Sushilla at the Chinese supermarket; not forgetting my old colleagues from the office (unless they're too tired maybe, or caught up in their grandchildren's homework, the preparations for another family wedding). Quite enough socialising to fill anyone's days, surely. Mary will be impressed by the number of friends I have. She's bound to be.

Yes, I know we'll get on fine. Like when we were kids. My poor little sister will soon learn to enjoy her vanilla tea as I have, and develop a fondness for mangoes, seafood and starfruit pickle. We'll go swimming every day, watch the flying fish while the air's still cool. If I listen carefully, I can hear myself even now, my voice lapping round her loving and warm as the waters of the lagoon.

'Cheers,' I say, raising my glass, 'to a life in paradise.'

Mary's stopped in mid-chew to stare at me. Then, slowly, her face lights up and she gushes, all excited and with her mouth full: 'Thank you, Tina, that's high praise indeed! I'm so glad you appreciate my efforts to keep the house looking its best: calendars make such a blessed difference. People can tell immediately they come in the door that *this* is a happy home.'

Thank God she's had to swallow at that point because I couldn't have held off much longer. 'Mary,' I shout, 'what on earth are you on about?'

A dark red stain is blossoming on the tablecloth between us where my glass should have been. Mary's eyes seem riveted to it; she's even moved her plate to get a better view. She has me really worried now: my own sister a crank! What if I'm too late already?

'Mary! You! Wake up! WAKE UP!'

At last she glances across, tentatively, almost furtively, though there's no reason to be afraid with me by her side. I want to hold her gaze but her eyes have slipped off and are fluttering round the room, straying from calendar to calendar like aimless butterflies.

'Mary, dear, you've lost touch,' I say, trying to sound affectionate, and reasonable. 'Listen: the world's out there, not in this house, not in calendars, not in your head. Out there. If you allow me, I'll show you.' I pause for an instant to let her say something. She is obviously too stunned with surprise – her eyes are very big and shiny, having come to rest on a spot over to my left.

'Mary? You've lived here too long, can't you see? It's time for a change now. You'll adore my island – everyone does. You might even find a job, at the local store perhaps, how about that? This place'll be easy to let: fully furnished, why, people'll jump at it! And you can always spend the odd holiday ... So don't you worry, Mary. It'll be wonderful to have you with me. To be together. Mary? Do you understand? We'll be together! On my paradise island!'

Mary's eyes have begun to hover between my face and that spot behind me, as if she can't quite detach herself from her cosy little fantasy world yet, can't quite make the leap across vast empty spaces to the reality of my island. Her lips are trying to shape a word, rounding themselves in vain, again and again, and she's shaking her head, overcome with confusion. I nod and smile encouragingly, then turn to take a look at what's so upsetting. Another calendar? Yes, this one's called Birds of Switzerland, dangling from the ceiling, twisting and untwisting on a piece of string – but all I can see pictured there is an ugly, tattered crow that seems to stalk backwards and forwards, backwards and forwards forever past something just out of focus.

~

Clowns, Clowns

She sat back in the armchair, crossing her legs. She'd allow herself one quick glance down, and that would be that. Sheer force of habit, really . . . But her thighs were so slender, with no fat and hardly a curve. And those hips! Almost narrow as a child's – Now, if she tucked her skirt in more tightly, yes, perfect, and folded her leg over just a little . . . No, she mustn't. Not tonight. What was she waiting for, anyway? The cassette recorder was ready; all she need do was press the red button.

The reels ground into action, the blank tape began to unwind and rewind, unwind and rewind, unwind and – How gentle that motion was. Round and round. How soothing. Impossible to look away. Such a pleasant tingling in her eyes. Then, all at once, twirls of darkness spinning into nothing . . .

She touched her forehead, fingered her eyelids. Had she nearly fainted again? Despite the yoghurt, the cups of fruit tea? Her hands started pulling at her fringe; swiftly, mechanically, they moved from left to right and back. Of course she wasn't going to faint – what nonsense! And she wasn't hungry either, not in the least. She'd merely let herself go for an instant. High time she got stuck in: the counter was simply gorging itself on numbers. She cleared her throat:

'Andreas, hi, it's me, your pen pal. I've decided to *speak* to you for a change. It's more fun than yet another letter and might help things along a bit. Sorry about the silence at the beginning – stage fright, no doubt . . .'

Such a ghastly acoustic in here. It made her sound all thin and tinny, a schoolgirl piping up from the tenth row. She tried lowering her voice: 'Just kidding. To be quite frank, I suddenly found myself travelling back in time, back to an afternoon at the circus long ago.' She paused; not bad, she was getting the hang of it now. 'Smack in the centre of the ring, the sand around him littered with small white balls, stands a clown, all anger and frustration. Wrong

guess – he isn't practising golf. Far from it. He's dying to say something, make a speech or tell a story, perhaps. But whenever he
opens his mouth a ball comes whizzing along, shutting him up yet
again. The audience's going wild; the plank seats are vibrating,
they're shaking . . . and I can't bear it any longer. Clenching my
fists and screwing up my eyes, I cry out, "Stop it, please, please, stop
it." Mother's laughing excitedly, saying in between claps not to be
silly, goodness me. Couldn't I take a joke for what it was? And
with her face towards Ann:"See that sister of yours? She'll never
learn to enjoy herself –"'

Shit, that wouldn't do, not as a starting point, anyway. She
flipped REWIND. The tape recorder belched, gave a little whine and
fell silent. Back at square one. She should take it easy, describe
her flat, maybe. Or she could ask him about Swiss summers; were
they hot enough, recommendable at all . . . ?

She forced herself to sit broadly, with both feet on the ground.
Three, two, one, zero . . . curtain up:'This is a spoken letter just for
you, Andreas. From you-know-who. Very personal, very special.'
She could feel giggles bubble up inside her, cool and glittering,
tickling her and – She held her breath, swallowed: 'Thanks for
returning the Celtic spoon I sent you for your birthday; you'd
prefer it engraved, I suppose . . . Oh, incidentally, did you receive
my Easter greetings? And the brochure on Scotland? The post's
terribly unreliable these days. Let me know, will you . . .'

Those bloody rats were running amok again. Squeaking and
squealing, rattling the metal bars of their cage, tearing at things.
It wasn't her fault the wee buggers had to diet, was it?
They couldn't even push through the circle of her thumb and
forefinger any more.

'Hear that racket coming from the kitchen? It's my pet rats.
Demolishing their new cardboard hut. Gratitude isn't one of their
redeeming features, I'm afraid. But how're you, Andreas? And
how's your Ph.D.? Both wilting in the Continental heat? I
bet you'll be working on a farm. Harvesting or, much better,

hay-making. The merest whiff of it so nourishing. Sweet and thick and spicy . . . You're not telling me you aren't trying to earn money for next term, are you? When I was a student we'd snatch at any job to keep ourselves in food and clothes. Just imagine the weight you'd lose as a farm labourer, and you'd be in the open too. A lot healthier than sliding about on the sweat marks in some gym.' She smiled down at herself. If she wanted to, she could span her stomach with one hand, one single starfish hand. Not sitting, of course. She'd need to lean back further, press her head deeper into the upholstery . . .

No, no, stupid, sit up straight. On with the show: 'Well, and – and if you have an afternoon off, most likely you'll go for a swim in the lake; in Switzerland there'd have to be a lake nearby, wouldn't there? Though perhaps it's too far to walk and you take your mountain bike instead. But that only makes you hotter, tauter, an arrow on a bow, quivering with eagerness, ha! ha! Even before you reach it, the water's rushing to meet you, its glassy waves surging up from the shadows, from the branches and leaves, the hollows between the roots; wads of algae shivering against your legs, wrapping round your ankles with small sucking noises like scratchy little cats' tongues . . .'

Another botch-up, for chrissakes. And him not exactly the easy-going type; he'd be certain to misconstrue . . . She slammed down STOP, then REWIND. She'd let him have part of it, '. . . -anches and lea- . . .' After all, she couldn't afford to spend the whole evening pussyfooting around '. . . -ween the roots'. Now:

'A hot summer – wishful thinking if ever there was. Up here it's cold, cold, cold. At the office this morning I had the fan-heater going. Yes, I'm still doing translations. Rather satisfying actually, a bit like . . . like cooking. Because you can peel words, squeeze words; you can chop them up and serve them plain; or you can fill them, blend them, bringing out subtle new flavours –'

Damn, her stomach had started to grumble again. She stifled it with her fists and continued: 'For the past few weeks I've been working on 'New Horizons in the Hoover World': everything from the performance ratings of suction nozzles to dustbag materials and shapes of body cavity. According to surveys women seem to favour the lightweights, the slimmest builds . . .' She chuckled, put her mouth closer to the microphone and whispered: 'Can you keep a secret? You see, I'm next in line for some advanced language courses abroad. My *Guide to Switzerland* tells me there're several towns in the southwest where both French and German are spoken. Sounds ideal, doesn't it? Places like Montreux, Fribourg, Neuchâtel, Something-de-Fonds . . . On the other hand, Alsace'd be nearer you –'

Bloody rats; why couldn't they stop banging away at their water feeder – or was it their bowls – for one second at least? Greed, sickening greed. But then, they were just animals and would never get beyond their animal instincts. She pressed PAUSE. Better fetch a cup of tea.

Good old Nutter was waiting for her, kicking at Pepper and biting into the wire mesh with yellow teeth. They'd done a neat enough job of their shoebox house: nothing left except a few piss-sodden shreds. They deserved a little reward. She raised the cage lid an inch, and out they shot like furious cannonballs, trailing flakes of onion peel and fluff across the kitchen lino.

'Hey,' she grabbed a bar of chocolate, ripped open the silver foil, 'here, you two!' Already they were charging towards her, pathetic creatures, with ears and nostrils flaring pink. She broke off a piece, started tossing it up in the air, higher and higher – 'C'mon, fatsos, on your hindlegs' – then suddenly flung it behind her. Nutter wheeled round at once, knocking Pepper over and butting him in the guts for good measure. She'd never fancied waltzing mice anyway; clowns were much more fun. She was going to train them, make them into stars. Be their ringmaster.

A second piece. A third.

No use; they were too dumb to catch anything. She gave a

low whistle and they came scuttling over, scrambled up her legs, her T-shirt, onto her shoulders . . . Pepper's tail was twitching against the nape of her neck, cold and hairless. Revoltingly hairless. Back into the cage with them, quick.

Afterwards she topped up their cereal and stuck a few slivers of carrot between the bars. Some cherry tea for herself, a whole big mugful.

She carried it back to the lounge, settled down into her chair again. So, roll out the tape and here goes: 'Hello, you still there, Andreas? I've just had my supper: chocolate and muesli. Thought I'd celebrate a little *à la suisse* . . .' She took a sip of tea, 'Mind you, the rats were pretty hungry. Haven't got used to reduced rations yet, poor souls, though it's in their best interest.' A long gulp – she felt nice and full now, her body glowing with warmth. 'Not that *I* am overweight.' She hastily smoothed down her skirt, moulded it to her thighs. 'On the contrary, people seem to enjoy looking at me.'

Her hands were up at her hair again, tugging gently to and fro. So many, many loose strands . . . She rubbed them between her palms, rubbed them coarse and crinkly, then dropped the tangles into the flowerpot nearby – that spider plant could do with a protein boost.

'Sorry about the gap, I was just remembering to get my hair cut. No, I'm not vain, don't be silly. I only said I've noticed getting noticed – pretty flattering for some of us – but I do my best to play it cool. Especially at the office. More than ever at the office, in fact. Who'd want to be in the limelight, tell me, with a crowd of bitching green-eyes watching my every move? So why the hell –'

The phone was ringing; its shrillness made her stomach jump like there was a yo-yo inside. 'I'm not going to answer it, don't worry. First come, first served.'

Maybe it *was* Neil, after all. To 'discuss matters further', as he'd promised. PAUSE. She left the tape wheezing in limbo and rushed through to the hall. Of course, she'd immediately picked up on his hidden agenda, she wasn't that naïve –

Too late. She'd be quicker next time.

Nutter and Pepper were bashing about like maniacs, shoving their snouts into the wire mesh with loud squeaks. The wee buggers just wouldn't leave her in peace, nipping at her fingers even when she was simply trying to keep them away from the rusty metal. She'd already played the 'chocolate game' with them – what more did they want?

Usually she didn't go in for big meals in the evening. Nothing worse than falling asleep on a heavy stomach; it gave you bad dreams. But tonight was a special occasion and her plate looked absolutely laden: cottage cheese half-oozing over the rim, a dam of cucumber-and-sweetcorn salad, and some Ryvita as a treat. She moved her chair up to the cage – the rats liked company – and started to eat, slowly. Very slowly. If she chewed everything properly she'd feel full afterwards. Wouldn't need to bring it all up into her mouth again, bring it up, chew and swallow it, over and over till her throat was rasping sore –

The phone. This time it could only be Mother. Mother who had a knack of phoning in the middle of meals. Who still thought of her as a babe in arms, coaxing her over to the restaurant where the 'wee snack' she'd prepared would turn into a frigging four-courser. That phone – the ringing itself was enough to make you puke. And those clowns beside her had better shut up – She swung her plate round and dumped the rest of the cottage cheese in the cage.

On her way to the lounge she unplugged the phone.

Now for her daily dozen, the homage to her daily bread. She pushed her skirt up above her waist and stood still, legs slightly apart, arms akimbo. Already her body was gaining momentum; she forced her hips round faster, the skin over her stomach tight as a drum. Faster, whirling the imaginary hoop up and down, round and round. So *alive* she was feeling, her muscles aching, her blood pulsing, more alive than ever, whirling, spinning . . . She'd landed on the floor, dizzy, sweaty and out of breath. Real shapeliness had its price, naturally.

She scrambled to her feet, swaying a little.

Back in her chair she switched off PAUSE and, for the briefest of moments, there was that wail again from the machine, high-pitched and tense, as if she'd released a trapped beast. She pressed her thighs together tightly: 'The last interruption, Andreas. Actually, I had another call just now. From Mother. Oh yes, she's fine, her old bustling self. Have I mentioned she's a cook? When my sister and I were small, she used to take us to work with her and we'd eat and play in a corner of the restaurant kitchen, have a nap there sometimes, right in the clatter and hiss, the greasy steam, the smell of frying onions, cabbage and bacon fat.'

She gazed out of the window. There were stacks of dirty dishes opposite, pots and pans boiling over, with black drips running down their sides . . . No. No, she must be hallucinating. She blinked. Pinched herself until it hurt. Until they were ordinary chimneys again.

'I can't be bothered to eat out much these days and, anyway, my job's the perfect substitute. Is that you shaking your head? Why don't you believe me? You'd be surprised at the number of letters in the alphabet whose shape suggests food. Indeed, I am surprised you haven't discovered this for yourself yet while researching that thesis of yours. What else are you doing but hunting for meanings, patterns? "T" looks like a table, doesn't it? A few "h"s around it, and you can get seated. Use your imagination, man! "O", never mind the plates and saucers, go for the real thing now, go for the nuts and olives, the rolls, the lamb medallions with peas and baby roasts, the toffee apples . . . It's a great game, don't you think? I've drawn up a list, everything in alphabetical order, with separate entries for lower and upper case, subcategories such as meat, dairy products, vegetables, fruit, eating utensils –'

Her voice had splintered and got caught in her throat, almost making her retch. Surely, none of those bitches could have seen the list? Or was that why they'd been whispering behind her back the last few days? She took a deep breath. Then another. No reason to get paranoid; nobody had ever laid eyes on the list except herself – just because Mother had begun spying on her didn't turn everyone else into snoopers.

'Yes, Andreas, I know: offices are breeding grounds for petty intrigues and jealousies. If gossip's the spice of life, we've had quite enough for a vindaloo recently. But as Indian food's my all-time favourite . . .' Such a good joke that; she sizzled with laughter and boxed her stomach back into silence. 'And it could just as easily have happened to one of the other girls – if they'd cared about their appearance a little more, shaped up better. Maybe one day, it will. Maybe one day Neil will invite *them* out for lunch. And what will *they* do then? Of course, the meal today was a mere pretext; Neil said he wanted to talk, and the way he glanced at me . . . He's in his late thirties, unmarried, handsome – and the boss. I sat listening to his voice, my head lowered so I wouldn't have to watch the worms of spaghetti slither and wriggle round the corners of his mouth. What a flatterer, though! He kept on and on about how slim I was, more fragile even than bone china. No wonder he didn't dare touch me; probably wants me in one piece, ha! ha! He was awfully anxious for me not to work "too hard", not to "overdo" things. Even mentioned a holiday – During the break this afternoon he came up to me, squeezed my arm and apologised for having been "so straightforward". *Straightforward!*' She nearly snorted. 'Then he said he'd like to meet up again to –'

What was the matter with Nutter and Pepper? She couldn't hear a sound, nothing at all. Lucky bastards must be high on cottage cheese. To be honest, she wouldn't mind a little something herself, recording was bloody tiring. Better cut it short now, bang in some music for a filler, and off to bed with a cup of blackberry tea.

'Time we chatted a bit more about ourselves. Well, Andreas, when will *we* be getting together? Your letters have become so few and far between I've finally got the message: you want a *proper* relationship. Blushing, are you? Listen, why would I have gone and inquired about those language courses otherwise? Or would you rather I asked for a transfer to the Continent right away? A real kick in the teeth for the hyenas at the office, and Neil cussing his damn reserve! I know what you're thinking. No, I haven't told Mother yet; now that sister Ann's set up home Down Under she wouldn't be too happy. We're pretty close, to say the least. – Which reminds me: how do you get on with your parents? See them often? Where do they live? What do they do? – Three measly letters, man, and the pages half-empty. No excuse for that, is there? Because you'll not be studying just now, only helping out some farmer. Easy enough to put pen to paper for ten minutes after work, I'd imagine. Or do you prefer spending your evenings in different company? Barbecuing sausages and chicken legs on lake shores? With some late night frolics in the water for dessert –? Well, I won't go on about it. Not me. I've even forgiven you for sending back that lovely Celtic spoon ... Sorry to bring this up. Sorry. Sorry. I didn't mean to. Really.

All I meant was to tell you about that clown I'd seen –
A clown, at the circus. The poor sod was trying to –
And whenever he opened his mouth –
Whenever he opened his mouth –
For fuck's sake, listen to me!
LISTEN! Whenever he –'

~

In Memoriam

Now that her mother is dead Celia has all the time in the world. No more fuzziness at the edges of days when late afternoon would blur into evening and evening into night, then midnight and finally early morning, with those cups of milky tea, bowls of soup and hot water bottles dripping and sloshing over the few remaining gaps between. From now on she'll sleep undisturbed, ten hours at least, and rip each day from the next in one clean tear.

A bit like yanking off the curtains in here a week ago, Celia thinks and looks up at the empty runner above the lounge window. She'd never taken to their grainy texture, their dirty skin colour. 'Silver sand' was what they'd been called in the catalogue, and her mother had stubbornly insisted on the term: 'Please, Celia, would you mind drawing the "silver sands", it's getting dark,' she'd whisper from the sofa if she wasn't too weak. A couple of nights after the funeral, while answering some letters of condolence, Celia had suddenly heard that voice again, like a slow tremble through the dusk. For once she hadn't hesitated. A few steps and she'd pulled, pulled as hard as she could. The fabric had spoken to her as it came away in her hands, shaking itself free from a decade's dust to cry out at last.

Time, of course, isn't the only thing Celia has in abundance now. There's the money, too. And space, yes, space most of all. Without warning it had exploded around her, expanding indefinitely until she could hardly see the corners of the room she happened to be in, as if the sharp winter sunlight had obliterated them, leaving her in the vastness of a desert. That's when she'd realised she'd better phone up some decorators.

Seven minutes past eleven; the man's late. Celia's eyes have slid away from the runner and are staring out into the street. The ash-tree in the garden's waving its pale bare branches at her as if to say, 'Nothing doing, nothing at all.' She pushes up the sash, leans out, willing the van to appear. She hopes the firm's name is emblazoned: 'Stillwell & Biggs, Decorators', spray-painted in colourful lunges to let the whole neighbourhood know that she, Celia Jones, is starting a new life.

She feels elated, and excited, because this is the first time she's ever made a decision that's bound to change things. *Things* as opposed to *ideas*. Things are visible, she believes; ideas and opinions can be hidden away. But now her moment has come. At last she'll be able to mar those creams and salmon pinks, those flaccid greens – the paint will stick, and so will the paste under the new wallpaper. Even steaming won't return the place to its previous state of unholy insipidness. Something will remain, she is sure. And that something will be hers and hers alone.

'Just don't say later I didn't warn you, Miss Jones.' It's five past twelve and the decorator, who had arrived in a van not unlike a hearse (jet black and polished to a gleam, with the firm's name curlicued discreetly in gold on both doors), sounds a little petulant. His professional pride has been hurt over and over, a room at a time, as it were. The woman's slightly off her rocker that's all, he consoles himself, or she wouldn't have clung to that nightmare of a colour scheme. Much too speedy she is, too eager to get it all over and done with in less than an hour, including tea or coffee and biscuits. He's worried. He's been through this kind of thing before: first the I-know-what-I-want rashness of choice, then – with the wallpaper still blistered and the paint still wet – the stunned silence, the murmurs of regret, shrill complaints, and acts of sabotage (sleek and wide-eyed and usually involving pets that always 'just happen to be moulting').

Celia doesn't bother to reply; words of caution no longer have power over her. She reaches for the order form on the coffee table, signs and dates it, her face glazed with obstinacy. Then, bringing out her cheque book, she suddenly relaxes, smiles towards the decorator: 'I'll pay two hundred now, if that's OK. The rest on completion of each room.'

'Suits me.' He nods, careful not to shake his head. While she writes out the cheque, he detaches the 'client's copy' from the form. Her signature's an almost-scrawl: 'Celia Jones', for God's sake! *Psychedelia*, more like! He closes the sample files, locks them in his briefcase with an extra loud snap. Then he brushes the biscuit crumbs off his trousers. A job's a job, after all.

A week from now the room they're in will be purple all over, various shades of purple to be precise. A lighter tone for walls and ceiling; the skirting, cornice, window frames and door surrounds a nuance darker; the shutters and doors darker still, with the inside panels near-black, like madly diminishing perspectives into some private hell.

It's the middle of the night, and Celia is awake. She forgot to pull the blind and cover up the chinks with the red scarf as usual, and now the moonlight is all over her. It's soaked into the bedding on top of her, underneath her, soaked into the folds round her head and feet, along her sides, making the sheets stiff and cold-heavy. She can't move, not even her little finger, just lies there and stares out at the huge frosty disk that's forced itself on her, stolen her sleep. Not a face, and certainly not a friendly one, whatever people might say. She can't think clearly because every now and again the disk becomes a gigantic eye that's trying to suck her into its brightness. After a while she begins to feel dizzy, and though she still can't move, it's as if she'd shrunk and was turning round and round inside those hardened sheets. To steady herself, she concentrates on the cloud shadows floating across the disk. But, by some incomprehensible trick of the atmosphere, the shadows themselves slowly dissolve into a ring of refracted light, a gigantic iris – tawny-orange, red, purple, bluey-green and yellow – to go with the gigantic white eye which has started sucking again, sucking, sucking her inside . . .

When Celia wakes in the morning, her left hand is clenched into a fist, her knuckles sore and bone-white, as if they'd been clasped round something for hours on end. She sits up, massages her fingers back into place, one at a time. That *something* was less than nothing, a bead of sweat perhaps, dried long since, or a dream she can't even remember.

Breakfast's a rushed affair today because she wants to get the clearing well under way before the decorator and his assistant drop off their tools and tins of paint in the afternoon. She's put on her oldest clothes, the pair of 'dove-grey' flares and the 'eau-de-nil' turtleneck (both presents from her mother, bought by mail order as 'a surprise' years ago and only ever worn if she'd been reminded). Passing down the narrow hall, Celia pictures the walls in crimson. That's the colour she'd selected yesterday, quite instinctively, without meaning to offend the decorator, who'd ended up making an impassioned stand for 'gentle gardenia' and 'the illusion of spaciousness'. Crimson, after all, is more than a mere colour to her, it's a feeling. It's the flush of anger on her mother's cheeks whenever she'd suspected her of loitering after teaching at the language school, going for a drive maybe or a visit to the cinema, instead of keeping her company. Homecoming *is* crimson for Celia, and always will be.

She pushes open the door to the lounge. She gasps. Reels. Falls to her knees. For the briefest of instants she'd glimpsed a figure draped on the sofa, extending an arm towards her.

What would her students say if they could see her now, so small and helpless, crouching on the floor? No doubt they're much too busy to spare a thought for her, the advanced group very likely screeching with laughter at Monty Python's 'Dead Parrot' sketch and all its synonyms for 'death'.

Celia's face feels gritty; her contact lenses itch and bite. She peels off her mother's beige Sunday gloves, soiled now beyond redemption, and pushes back her hair. She'd never have believed a carpet kept so scrupulously clean, vacuumed at least once a week, could produce such a flurry of dust and fluff. The room seems to be swirling with it, to have grown darker, more distinct, as if its ceiling, walls and corners had hauled in the space between them, compressing it, like a snow cloud that's closing in on a winter's day.

She's ripped up a good two thirds by now, pulling out the carpet staples with a claw hammer. One of them, near the fireplace, had stuck so fast she'd lost her balance and staggered back against the sofa; the hammer had missed her by inches and instead gouged a hole in her mother's favourite silk cushion. Another of her selfish whims, Celia thinks, staring down at the floor: a white carpet in a room with a live coal-fire.

Her mother'd had it fitted shortly after Father left them, 'to find his luck elsewhere', as she'd explained. The phrase has lodged in Celia's mind like a precious stone – when she was little, she used to associate it with 'that man' or 'Daddy', picture him mining for gold and diamonds, far away; now that she's grown up and learnt to deal with abstracts she asks herself at times: 'Once you've lost it, whatever *it* is, how do you know where to start looking?'

Celia still remembers the day of her first real date and how nervous she was, so nervous a big lump of coal fell off the scuttle and bounced a smudge trail across the white carpet, yards beyond the tidily laid-out newspapers. She'd done her best to conceal the stains temporarily – it *was* an emergency, after all – regrouping the armchairs, the coffee table and the standard lamp, scattering a few books on the floor, spine-up, as if for further reference. Then, dressed in her purple trouser suit with lipstick and eye shadow to match, her hair combed one last time in front of the hall mirror, she'd been reaching for the spare set of keys on their hook by the door –

'Oh, before you're off, Celia, dear: I noticed a small mishap in the lounge . . .' Smiling her cleanest smile, her mother had held out a basin of soapy water, a toothbrush and several sheets of blotting paper, pale blue blotting paper.

'I'm really sorry, Mother. I'll sort it when I get back. Promise.'

'This isn't a coalmine, Celia.'

'Honest, I promise.'

'Which only leaves me, doesn't it . . . ?'

She'd been three quarters of an hour late, and her young man long gone. Ever since, Celia's hated that bland soggy blotting-paper blue; she never walks to the school now if the sky's that colour, she either drives or takes the bus. On such days she waits for night to come like the spread of a dark cloth.

Celia squeezes her mother's gloves back on, rumbles the furniture over onto the floorboards, and sets to tearing off the rest of the carpet, kicking and rolling it up into a slumped kind of shape. It's too heavy to shift, a leaden weight with none of its former springiness left. She'll be glad to see it carried out of the house to be burnt or dumped in one of those landfill sites.

The floorboards and the dirt gaps running straight and black in between seem to give the lounge direction at last. As if it was free to move now, might, indeed, at any moment incline slightly towards the ash-tree in its patch of wizened grass out front or, especially of an evening, retreat through the next room into the peace of flowerbeds, birds and clothes-lines at the back.

'That should come off easily enough,' the decorator says, sliding his knife sideways under the champagne wallpaper next to the door surround. 'See?' He half-turns to Celia, then tugs sharply and pulls off a strip, exposing a sea-green mural underneath, complete with whorls of blue, yellow and red like tropical fish. He brandishes the paper strip but Celia's no longer paying any attention. She's gone up to the wall and started tracing the different colours with her fingernail, up, down, left, right, round and round and round.

Celia imagines the new roundabout a few blocks away. She loves driving with the steering wheel at near-full lock, loves the sense of comfort it gives her, particularly after lessons on word order or the sequence of tenses. She'd managed a record seventeen circuits, traffic and all, the day her mother died. If it hadn't been for the strain to her eyes and a sudden numbness creeping up her legs, she could have gone on forever.

The decorator's assistant brushes past with a stepladder and some dustsheets. She doesn't seem to notice, and for a moment he watches her finger drawing circles on the bare patch of wall, his eyes hooded from years of guarding against splashes of paint, loose flakes of plaster and wallpaper, and single ladies who want their immaculate flats shredded then re-padded for no reason that he can see, except perhaps to keep themselves busy, and entertained. With a shrewd, well-rehearsed glance-and-grin towards his boss he says:

'That green colour's nothing special, just ancient paste. You get it in most old houses. You'd be surprised, though, at some of the other things we find under wallpaper. Isn't that so, Colin?' Here he forces open his lids, raises his voice a notch. 'Like that time over at the manor house, remember?' The woman's hand doesn't stop, never even slows down; she reminds him of the black cat he had as a boy and how it used to sit behind the closed door, pawing and pawing to be let in.

The decorator, meanwhile, has crossed to the fireplace, knife in fist, and stabbed the wall high up, slicing off another strip, expertly, right down to the skirting. He has decided to play along for a bit, not really to humour his assistant nor to tease the woman either – he's not the teasing sort – but because she annoys him, plain and simple, annoys him standing there, ignoring them like they're a couple of dummies. He looks over his shoulder and calls out, rather loudly, 'No dark secrets here, Rob. Not yet, at any rate . . . !'

Celia is aware, of course, that she's being watched and ridiculed, only she couldn't care less. It's just like writing something on the blackboard with one's back to the class. She can do what she wants now, can't she? And if she feels like stroking the wall she'll damn well do it. The surface has a waxy sheen that makes her think of skin . . . Such schoolboy jokes, anyway: do they expect her to be bothered about ghosts and things? About dead mice and rats, wing–cases of beetles stuffed into wall holes?

Abruptly, Celia swivels round to face the two men, who, she notices with a certain teacherly relish, jump into action at once, flapping their dirty white dustsheets over the bookshelves, armchairs, sofa and coffee table, stacking rolls of paper, tools and tins into neatly useless pyramids. She is getting impatient; they can do all this tomorrow, it's half past four now and they promised not to keep her. A gleam of metal catches her eye.

'Excuse me,' she says, and stoops to pick up the stripping knife, its handle faintly warm still, 'may I borrow this?'

She'd laughed out loud at their sheepish, scandalised looks, at the threat in the decorator's voice when he wished her 'a pleasant evening' from the doorstep. Afterwards, like a good girl, she'd put the knife back down because she doesn't really need it, does she? Celia leans her head against the painted coolness of the open lounge door. Her eyes have started to water, she's laughed so much.

'You don't blink enough, that's what's wrong with you,' the optician had told her last week. She had gone to see him a few days after the funeral, because of the bleary featurelessness she'd begun to experience in the flat. What a sad man he must be to want people to blink all the time, she'd reflected and smiled to cheer him up. In response he'd taken hold of her head, squirting something from a bottle straight into her eyes: 'Come on, Miss Jones. Blink!' And again, his voice split with impatience: 'Blink! I said. BLINK! BLINK!'

And now Celia's blinking and blinking, and it doesn't help. Not one bit. The room's a liquidy blur and already the walls are receding. The dustsheets are looming larger and brighter, with an unbearable hint of blue leaking from their folds, as if they had blotted up too much daylight. Celia wants to shut the door and walk away, but there's that cold-heavy weight again all round her, like last night. Blink by blink the clutter of furniture beneath the dustsheets changes shape, its jagged outlines slacken, level out, merge into one single mass, more and more familiar; and although she knows this is impossible, she can see it just the same, right in front of her: that oblong object, shrouded.

Celia blinks and blinks. If she blinks long enough, the room will settle down – she's got all night. If she blinks long enough, the furniture won't pretend to be anything but furniture, and she'll be fine. All the time in the world. She'll blink and blink, waiting for the rustle as the sky's turned inside out.

~

Inside ~ Outside,
or: Playing Baba Yaga

The photo slithers from the envelope almost stealthily, and he doesn't touch it. So this is Zoe. If he didn't know better, he'd think she was on holiday, getting her picture taken in some public park. She's laughing and resting one foot against the stone base of a fountain, her right hand poised above her head as if she's about to smooth down her hair. She's laughing at him, it seems, or rather at the sight of him having breakfast in a room that can't be much larger than a prison cell, with its table jostling the baby grand (his prize possession) and the baby grand half-straddling the mattress on the floor.

Simon's always hated women posing like this, trying to appear casually innocent when underneath the cream-coloured shorts and blouse it's all murderous strength. She is wearing sandals, and her toenails are painted the same shade as her lips. Her eyes are a shivery green, like seaweed caught between rocks.

She looks nowhere near as crazy as the newspapers had made her out, a year or so back. But certainly nothing like the voice either, the little-girl telephone voice he's come to know only too well over the past couple of months.

~

Of course Zoe isn't poking fun at anyone, least of all you, young man. Can't you guess how hard it must be for her to conjure up that smile, lift that arm of hers like she's going to pull a rabbit from some invisible hat when all she feels is a familiar lurch of self-disgust? Afterwards she'll rush to one of the bright red benches arranged like screams along the paths; she'll sit kicking at the gravel they'll get her to rake over again this evening, glaring now at the wall of trees opposite, now at the clots of freshly cut grass that soil the ground to her right and left. She'll ignore the woman with the camera a few steps behind her.

This is one of the rare hot days of sunshine, so in a little while she'll calm down; she'll remember the mauve writing pad she's brought with her intending to make the most of being outside – for as long as they let her. And that's when she'll remember *me*, still standing a little way off, patient and discreet (and happy now I've safely captured her on film); she'll remember me with gratitude, invite me to come and sit beside her, help her put the usual finishing touches to one or two letters. Without *me*, and she knows this as plainly as I do, she'd never have been allowed to stay out here more than a quarter-hour. Watching over her has its own appeal – and rewards. There are possibilities with her, definite possibilities.

~

Simon pours himself a cup of tea, then props Zoe's photo against the marmalade jar. The sun's burst into the room all of a sudden, throwing the glossy surface back at him. Can this really be the girl who's been calling him? Writing to him? She's pretty, no doubt, but also pretty shifty-looking. A bit of a bitch, in fact. He gulps down some tea, burning his mouth.

The first time Zoe had phoned he wasn't in and she left a message on his answering machine.

'Hello, Mr Campbell,' she'd said in a whisper, and he'd imagined someone lying asleep next to her, a baby perhaps, or a lover ... 'My name's Zoe. I saw the review of your Mozart recital in the paper the other day and just wanted to say CONGRATULATIONS! Wish I could have been there myself! Maybe speak to you later in the week ... Bye for now.'

Harmless flattery, he'd thought then.

Simon realises he's still staring at the photo, at one of its corners more precisely, just above her raised arm, where the tree branches don't quite reach and a half-inch of sky presses against the blurred gleams of high wire fencing. Is that why she's put up her arm, to pretend that blot on the landscape – and on her own life – isn't there?

~

'All I want is OUT and because I can't get OUT I must learn to put up with it' – this is how Zoe rationalises her status quo, telling me every so often. She puts her case rather bluntly, wouldn't you say? And not just that, but it sounds like an incantation, like she's trying to draw a magic circle around herself. I do feel for her, especially when she has that sincere, anxious look on her face. A look I treasure more than anything, perhaps for its very nakedness – figuratively speaking, as it were. She's prone to forget her own reasoning, though, and to start raving on and on about how the whole thing that brought her here was an 'accident', a terrible 'accident' – wasn't she the prime witness, after all? And that's where I come in: I have to keep her right. I have to teach her to live with guilt. Which doesn't necessarily mean accepting it, you'll understand. There are other ways –

~

It must have been nearly a fortnight before he had heard from Zoe again, late one evening. By then he'd performed his programme in several other cities and she'd become one of many callers, guileless enthusiasts mostly (as he regarded her, too, at that stage) – apart from a few would-be musicians who began trying to ensnare his better self with sob stories, like he was some sort of agency. Still, that's how he'd got to know Lesley. She was an exception, of course – even over the phone there could be no mistaking the cheeky maid Susanna, straight out of *Figaro*.

So when the phone rang he'd expected it to be Lesley and made a quick grab for the receiver, leaning across the table and knocking over a quarter-full bottle of red.

'Hello? Hello? Is this Simon Campbell, please?'

At the sound of the whisper voice he covered the mouthpiece and cursed, wondering briefly whether to cut her off. But he was Mr Nice Guy, and she a woman.

'Yeah. Hello.' Rain had begun to fall, marking the window beside him with long, silvery cracks.

'It's Zoe. You probably won't remember me —'

He didn't want to commit himself and forced a laugh, 'Well, if you could turn the volume up a fraction . . .'

She giggled, then explained, hardly any louder, that she was doing something forbidden. She'd managed to get at one of 'their' phones with a little inside help, because she'd been 'good' (apparently, she'd played the piano for 'them'). She loved playing the piano. And she'd really been impressed by —

The dry rustle of her words was beginning to grate. 'Listen —' he interrupted, as calmly as possible, and felt like adding, 'nutcase', '— why're you telling me all this? Who are you? I'm pretty busy, you know.' He drew the fingers of his free hand through the puddle of wine on the table and started to lick them off one by one; once he'd finished she could go to hell — if she wasn't there already.

Instead of answering him she seemed to consult someone, then, abruptly, the dialling tone came on. *She*'d hung up.

He'd felt vaguely guilty. And pissed off. So, having poured what was left of the wine, he took a good swallow and set the glass on top the baby grand. He needed something loud now, *forte fortissimo*, to clear his ears from that rustling voice of hers, something like Mussorgsky's Great Gate of Kiev in *Pictures at an Exhibition* or, much better, the Baba Yaga movement. But his hands had chosen without him and were already chasing a Bach fugue up and down the keys. They were gaining on it fast, accelerating relentlessly, till the notes seemed to blur to a standstill. Miss Gleeson, his first piano teacher, would have been proud of him . . .

The next moment the chase was over, the fugue crawling along like a funeral march.

And once again it was years and years ago. One of those blind November evenings. He was waiting for Miss Gleeson's customary triplet ring at the door, wishing – as he had for weeks, ever since she'd begun plaguing him with her finger exercises – that she wouldn't turn up this time, thanks to an overeager pupil perhaps or the weather or, best of all, some sudden virulent disease. Miraculously, his wish seemed to be granted: there was no triplet ring that night – or any other night afterwards. Miss Gleeson, his parents told him, had been killed on the way to their house; a hit-and-run accident. At first he'd felt a rush of relief. But then the whisperings started, a voice inside him like dead leaves, insinuating things. As if it had all been *his* doing. As if *he* was to blame. Throughout the rest of his childhood the memory of her had haunted him and he couldn't stop playing, playing, playing.

Now, fifteen years on, Simon knows of course how stupid he'd been at the time. A small boy locked in his guilty conscience. Naïve, really. Thoughts can't kill, after all. And yet, with Zoe's photo less than a foot away, he can feel just a whiff of the old fear rising like damp inside.

~

Whether Zoe believes me or not is neither here nor there, as long as she does what I tell her. And I tell her she ought to forget – no use in crying over spilt milk. That's how I got her to read the newspaper and mark whatever items she thought interesting. Then the first thing my sweet girl snags on is that picture of you in concert at the City Hall.

'See him?' she said, 'He's nice. He's got a kind of rugged handsomeness, sharp and dreamy – and his hands look like the hands of a good man.'

I just nodded, didn't want to sway her either way, which was pretty fair, considering. Because I knew the instant I set eyes on you that you'd be perfect for what I had in mind, absolutely perfect. Nervy fingers are always a giveaway, of course. And names: 'Simon Campbell' sounds much too bland to be true.

Getting hold of your address and number was a piece of cake: a quick search through the computerised phone books while I was updating my Progress Reports later that day. In my file on Zoe I noted: 'Intends to embark on pen friendships with people OUTSIDE, as a means of keeping in touch with what she calls "reality" – rehabilitation process initiated by inmate herself.'

How disappointed Zoe was not to catch you in, that first time she rang. I'd rigged it all up for her, smuggled her near a phone when she should have been in her cell, alone, before lights out. Her disappointment was so acute I felt I had to comfort her with a hug, one of those butterfly hugs – mere show and no substance – which was as far as she'd go physically, the poor traumatised lovely (though she's become a little more trusting since, you'll be glad to hear). Then I said in my crispest guard's tone: 'OK, Zoe, one more call.' She smiled and held out her hand towards me, palm up: 'You choose, please,' and I chose from the list of names and numbers written like so many smudges across her life-line.

You see, Simon, you're not the only one. Zoe would never want to put all her eggs in one basket again, not after what she's been through. She picked three others from the paper that day besides you: there's the victim of a racist attack, rather handsome – if you like them ebony; then a young male ballet dancer she couldn't resist (no harm in him, I suppose); and, last but not least, the stand-up comic Cara Davis – vociferously independent-spirited, yet, by the look of her, the kind of lady who'd just love to have a pretty girl like Zoe curl up in her lap.

So don't you flatter yourself.

~

Simon can't forgive Zoe for sending him the picture. She has no right to thrust her appearance at him like that. It makes her so offensively real. Why couldn't she simply remain the voice floating down the phone line? Or the handwriting on mauve notepaper, precise and regular enough to have been printed by a machine? Why on earth did she have to become *someone* at all?

Outside, a blackbird has burst into one of those piercing, syncopated rhapsodies that always remind him of Lesley, his perky little Susanna. Lucky he'd warmed to *her* sob story (soprano in her second year with no money and no experience as a performer outside the conservatoire, but dying to be taught a thing or two). He wonders what she's doing just now. Chatting up her singing teacher, maybe? Or sitting close to a girlfriend, giggling over the pros and cons of screwing to *Boléro*? Thank Christ Lesley isn't pretending like *this* one; he sneaks another glance at the picture. With Lesley he has fun: fun rehearsing, fun at the table, eating and drinking, fun under the table, under the baby grand . . . With Zoe – He knocks the photo over. Feels like giving its waxy white back a slap with his knife but whacks off some butter instead, spreading it on a piece of toast in short rasping strokes. The blackbird has broken off in mid-song and there's only the sound of tyres on cobblestones now, a low drumming beat that hardly varies in intensity, insidiously hypnotic.

A phrase comes into his head, the stupid, clichéd phrase Zoe used in one of her recent letters. Round and round it goes: 'I'm not a monster, Simon, not a monster.' While finishing his tea and toast he psyches himself up for his practice session, tapping out various rhythms on the table top. Driving them hard and vicious like the Baba Yaga piece.

When Zoe called again, after a sulky silence that lasted several days, he'd done his best to be patient with her. And firm: No, unfortunately he was too busy to undertake more teaching, sorry about that. Perhaps later some time (in other words: never). She seemed content enough just to discuss music, which he didn't mind overmuch – though her favourites, Schubert and

Brahms, are rather on the heavy side. Once or twice he'd actually played her some passages and she had to guess what they were. Music apart, he's kept himself out of things.

Simon grimaces; the marmalade's left a bitter taste in his mouth, like a sneer trapped inside. His hands are still hammering out their rhythms on the table top and he is thinking about Baba Yaga, Mussorgsky's witch. Picturing the wall that's supposed to surround her hut – even as a boy it was her wall he'd found most alluring – and how the bones and skulls it's made of blaze in the dark.

~

Still, Simon, you're the reason why Zoe took up the piano again, with a vengeance. She must have fallen for the sound of your voice, the silly thing, certainly not for your manners, if you'll excuse me. She can be such a romantic at times. Anyway, one free minute, even during the short breaks from work which the other girls fill in with gossip, and she's off like a shot to the recreation room. I love watching her play – yes, young man, 'watch' *is* the right word, because Zoe is quite a sight when she's at it, with her hands and hair and breasts sliding all over the keyboard as if to placate the demons she can't command. Not much longer now and she'll be ready – game for anything, I hope.

To be quite frank, no one here's really bothered about the quality of her music (or knows much about it, for that matter), the dear girl's got that wrong, I'm afraid. But as long as she's happy playing, we're happy watching.

You for your part have been playing along rather nicely and if I could, I'd thank you for it (you're one of the best genies I've ever had, which is saying something). Quite magical, the way you made that first phone conversation dry up just as she'd started to gush on about you and your concerts again. She was annoyed with *me* afterwards, would you believe, for advising her to ring off.

'Why can't I simply tell him? Tell him everything?' she kept asking as we sneaked back to her cell. Why indeed!

Zoe means well, Simon, don't forget that. You mustn't lose your temper too soon.

~

Then, about four weeks ago, Zoe had got him at an all-time low. He was bogged down in his arrangement of scenes from Saint-Saëns's *Samson and Delilah* for piano and two voices, Lesley's and Mike's, bogged down in a quagmire of keys and notes and ornamentation. To make things worse, Zoe didn't seem to be in the mood for the usual music talk and spoke with a breathy kind of swagger as if to challenge him, moaning on about her piano teacher at primary school and how she'd had to analyse each and every piece before being allowed to play. Miss Gleeson all over again. He was about to hang up when he heard her say:

'You see, Simon, I've always trusted my instincts and done the thinking later.'

There was a confused bustle, then more whispers, velvety as ever but unexpectedly defiant:

'The world's full of people planning for the width and height of their private treadmills, not even leaving the choice of their coffins –'

'So that former boyfriend of yours,' he cut in, trying to get his own back at last, 'the one you killed as you implied recently, was in fact *saved*, is this what you're saying? Saved by manslaughter from a boringly predictable life – and death?'

The fury of her response took him by surprise: she'd shrilled abuse down the line till he had enough and put the phone down. Even afterwards her cries kept ricocheting in his ears.

Sounding more and more familiar. Like Miss Gleeson during their lessons when he was a kid. Miss Gleeson shrieking for the scissors as his ragged, untrimmed nails scurried and scuttled across the piano lid she'd made him close 'for the finger exercises'. She had a horror of mice and rats, she'd once told him, of their sharp little feet, their sharp little teeth, and he'd begun to exploit this. Perhaps she'd give in one day and let him play real music from start to finish rather than waste time practising those hollow grace notes and triplets, sextolets, *legato* and *staccato*, to the clacking of the metronome.

No, he had reflected when the ringing in his ears eased off, no, Zoe wasn't the only one with a hateful Miss Gleeson. With hateful memories. But that's where the similarities ended. Zoe's piano teacher didn't get herself run over. And killed. Didn't die on the way to a pupil who'd wished her dead.

~

A little extra indulgence from me, Simon, and Zoe will be weaned from you for good. She's fairly tractable, after all, despite those occasional fits of passion. See, she has stopped kicking the ground now; there's no gravel left where she is sitting, only bare earth, slashed and double-slashed by her feet. Of course, I'll pretend not to notice – there is a time for everything – and pick up her writing pad instead.

'How about some letters of invitation, Zoe? Why not ask your pianist friend to visit?' I'll say, tongue-in-cheek. Because we know already, don't we, that she won't stand a chance when it comes to the crunch. Except that you did rather overstep the mark the last time she phoned and found you in.

I'd pepped Zoe up specially for that call, told her to try and have a real conversation with you for a change, a conversation about herself, her own life, not just dead composers and their fusty scores. Naturally, I counted on you to spoil it for her. But surely, Simon, your musician's ear ought to have picked up on the difference in pitch when *I* took the receiver to deliver that little spiel of mine about treadmills. We could have spared her some of your resentment at least (remember, it's not time yet for the grand *finale*), and I wouldn't have needed to swear at you quite so much, nor to suffer her wrongful accusations, seeing that I'd been on her side all along, like a true fairy godmother.

Oh yes, she was mad. Mad at my 'stupid interference', my 'thickness' – hadn't I realised she was just about to explain herself to you? The poor child even attempted to rush off to her cell without me! I had to throw my arms right round her in a tight embrace and not let go (and if my hands did stray a little in the heat of the moment, what of it? *She* never noticed anyway, being far too upset). It took quite a while to reach a compromise: I suggested helping her write up an 'eyewitness account' of the 'accident' (with the necessary imaginative dimension – for the human interest, as it were), to be dispatched to you first thing, and she promised to try and be friends again ('kiss and make up' was how I put it).

But tell me, Simon, why this constant urge of people to confess? Why is *once* never enough? Guilt is one thing, masochism quite another. 'You can't undo the past, Zoe,' I keep reminding her, 'just leave it be. If anything, build on it!'

The sun has gone in and the trees by the perimeter fence seem to be crowding closer all of a sudden, their foliage near black as they push their way towards us. Zoe remains motionless, as if under a spell. I reach for the camera round my neck. She looks so forlorn on that bench, so adorably forlorn, only the back of her head is visible from here. For a breathless second it feels like I'm one of those curving red bench slats, clutching and clasping her body. Then she turns. She must have heard the *click*.

'Just finishing the film, my dear, so we can get your pictures back more quickly.' I give her a hasty smile and start fiddling with some levers for emphasis. She eyes me silently, steadily, until I've sat down. There's mud between her toes, and the nail varnish is chipped.

'Why can't I be left alone ever,' she says without inflecting her voice, without a glance even, as if addressing the cloud that's taken the sunshine away from her.

But when I touch her, she doesn't draw back.

~

Two days after Zoe's abuse down the phone he had received the first of those mauve letters (mauve to mollify him, presumably?), a description of 'what really happened a year ago'. *Her* version of the truth, at any rate.

Lesley is always telling him he's too hard on Zoe, but he wonders what she'd say to this photo now, or to last week's letter urging him to visit, please, please, please – it was so terrible to be shut away from the rest of the world, especially if you loved life and people ('human beings in particular' was added in brackets, complete with a couple of exclamation marks).

Until two weeks ago Lesley didn't even know Zoe existed, let alone where she stayed, and why. It had been late afternoon; he and Lesley were licking chocolate ice-cream off each other – ice-cream for afters, so to speak. By now they were well past the *Boléro* stage and screwed in their own time, in every sense.

'From Ravel to Pavlov,' he joked, letting his tongue hang out.

Lesley laughed and, as a reward, took a few yelping snaps at it; meanwhile, her hands strayed down his belly:

'How about another wag of the tail then?'

At that moment the phone started to ring. He wasn't worried because as usual when Lesley was around he'd made sure to switch on the answering machine. Only he hadn't reckoned on the volume being up and that whisper voice suddenly filling the room, saying:

'Hi Simon, it's me, Zoe. How're you today? I've been dream-ing of your playing night and day almost . . .'

He got up in a hurry to silence it. Too late, though; Lesley was already wrenching on her jeans. He followed her to the door, covering himself with his hands: 'Hey, wait a minute! It's not what you're thinking, not in a million years. I've never met the woman. She's just one of . . .'

She wheeled round. Her eyes seemed to fizz and when she spoke, her words vibrated, her 's's hissing and wet: 'Yeah, just one of your slavering groupies! Just like me!'

She tried to slam the door in his face but he caught hold of it: 'Lesley, chrissakes, don't go!' Throwing on the nearest coat, he went flashing after her down the stairs. 'She's in fucking jail, Lesley.' He hadn't meant to tell her and it felt like a betrayal. Then like a curse:

'Jail, Lesley. Jail. She's in jaaaiiiiiil!' The long-drawn-out vowels spiralled wildly down the stairwell and eventually he heard her footsteps getting slower, till there was only his breath and the scrape of dirt on stone as he reached the bottom. And reached out for her where she stood hovering, her face turned away, between belief and disbelief.

Later, after the reconciliation under the baby grand, he had shown her Zoe's 'confession':

It was Saturday night and we'd been invited to a party. Ralph was having a bath while I was blow-drying my hair. I hadn't dressed yet. Suddenly he pointed at me and shouted:

'Hey Zoe, what the hell's that?'

'What do you mean, "that"?' I said. Usually, he never noticed a thing, except carpets, rugs and knots per square inch, or other women. I carried on doing my hair, brushing and stroking and draping it like a cat round my shoulders.

'Come on now, Zoe, don't play games. You're pregnant, aren't you? The way you're standing there – fucking pregnant!' He slammed down his fist and the bathwater splashed all over the place:

'I don't want a fucking brat. I told you, didn't I? Didn't I?'

Suddenly he's halfway out the bath and yanking my head back by the hair:

'Answer me!'

'You bastard!' I hit out, hair dryer and all. Next thing I know he's let go of me with a yell and crashed back into the bath. The water spray-guns round him, he screams and flails and there's a bang, a flash, and a smell like the burnt-out motor of a washing machine. He's gone limp and silent. I can't move.

His eyes were the worst. They still are. At night I wake to find them, unblinking and bright like a wild beast's, looking in at me through the bars on the window. And often during the day I feel his shadow there. It's between me and the light, growing bigger all the time and thicker, strangling the sky outside.

PS. I had the baby aborted as soon as they let me.

~

I'm in charge of recreations tonight. The room's heavily dosed with muzak to hold tempers at bay; we don't want our inmates to start fighting at this time of night – though personally, I've nothing against the occasional fight, especially when the girls revert to plain, hard and honest body work (something I'll have to teach Zoe: the art and joy of grappling). As usual, both tellies are on, a wail of sirens in one corner, the tinsel laughter of some studio audience in the other. I'm at the far end, beside the CCTV screen that shows the games room downstairs.

From behind the sliding partition nearby come the muffled sounds of Zoe playing something slow and soulful. She's pining, Simon. That's why she's shut the rest of us out. Pining. Don't you feel even the slightest twitch at your heartstrings? There's my little lovely, responding to that venom of yours with a confession, then leaving the odd message on your answering machine, dropping the odd line, inviting you here; and from you – nothing. Just silence.

'Check!' cries a voice to my right. I jerk round but it's only Margery. Margery who's so fat she occupies two chairs and is always getting bossed about by dark and slinky Karen, though no doubt it's her that's got the brains. I smile at them and Margery smiles back. Karen frowns, glowers at me, then turns away in a pointed manner to realign the chessmen on the board. An intriguing couple, wouldn't you say?

What's happening to Zoe? Her music seems to have got unhinged all of a sudden, its rhythm lurching and squint somehow. There's no time to lose: this is it, the haunted hour. A glance across the room, another at the screen, but none of the girls seem to have noticed a thing, or to be paying any attention; they continue with their games and gossip, continue sprawling in front of the tellies. Discreetly, I slide the partition open – and closed.

She must have heard me come in because of the way she starts flinging her body around on the stool. She's bursting with blood, Simon, I can tell. And she wants me; even if only by default, she wants me. Badly. No more butterfly hugs, or butterfly kisses. No one can live on hope, or fear, forever. She carries on playing as I go up to her from behind. She'll have to carry on playing now because stopping would break the spell. My belly presses into the hollow of her back, my fingers probe the stringy, vibrating flesh between her neck and shoulders, and she sighs, her head flailing up against my breasts. When I lean over, she lifts her face towards me, lifts it higher and higher. Yes. Yes, she wants me. Badly.

~

What a snake she is, what a snake of a woman; Simon's picked up the photo again and is staring at it, holding it at arm's length as though to demonstrate to himself how Zoe fills him with repulsion. No wonder that boyfriend of hers had wanted to keep her out of harm's way, keep her safe in her own snake basket – a very luxurious one, by the sound of it, lined with the thick

Persian carpets he'd dealt in. 'My first cell,' Zoe had once said, 'was padded for comfort.' She must have been spoilt to the core right enough. Why else complain about not having to go out and earn her crust, complain about lunching in '*chic*-erias' where quail-egg *consommé*, nasturtium salad and ostrich steak were *tables d'hôte*? She ought to have thanked her lucky stars! That guy even bought her a Steinway. A fucking Steinway! Meanwhile people like himself have to start off on a tenth-hand piano with grimy ivories, have to pay their way through the conservatoire and master classes tutoring people just like her, people so bloody cocooned they lose sight of what it's like on the wrong side of town.

Simon shoves the photo under the stack of newspapers on the table, scrunches the envelope into a ball. Now for some Scarlatti, pronto, pronto; his stuff's great for loosening up fingers and setting knuckles ablaze. That's what he tells his pupils too (he's kept five of them, selected chiefly on their financial merit. Concert careers have been known to go wrong before, and those few recent successes and big write-ups are no insurance against future losses).

'Fire,' he'd say to them, and it's one of his most effective lines, 'is the breath and life of music. You have to feel its heat inside you when you play. You have to make the score glow and crackle with it. You have to make the hearts of your listeners burn.' Then, after the obligatory dramatic pause, he'd strike the topmost keys to finish off:

'Without fire every single note will freeze under your hands, and die.'

Little lies like these work wonders, Simon knows. They boost the self-confidence, help create a sense of urgency. And if a pupil's at all gifted he'll soon realise they're just teaching-tricks, that some pieces need to be rendered with coldness because only coldness can show off their brilliance, their glittering surface of ice-hardness.

Simon feels ready for the Saint-Saëns now; plenty of time for a run-through before the rehearsal with Mike and Lesley at half two, provided she manages to sneak out of Music Theory, of course. But then, she *is* one for practice – makes a ravishing Delilah even out of bed. Mike's proved quite a find too: excellent tenor, good fun and, most convenient, not bothered about women. When Lesley suggested he let his hair grow for the part, he'd simpered in a mock-*castrato*: 'Oh, but my boyfriend would never allow that, he'd think I'd become a raging queen.'

~

After last night, Zoe and I are almost friends. Almost close friends. But she still craves for people from OUTSIDE, and that's why I need you, Simon – or rather, your patience – a little longer.

So here we are next to the phone once more. Thank God you're home! Zoe's glowing and talking in a low voice, leaning up against the wall. She still believes in you, still hopes you'll be the one to free her from her enchanted life inside the magic circle, little guessing I've reserved this pleasure for myself. Give me a few more days, a week at most, and you'll be rid of her, I guarantee.

You see, Cara Davis, the stand-up comic, has announced a visit. Shortly. She's keen, I can tell. Such fluttery, flowery writing you'd think her words would burst into sticky bloom the moment your eyes flit over them. Dead keen. The woman's salivating at the prospect of a nice little toy girl safely tucked away behind bars.

And this is where you come in, Simon –

'Yes, fine. I'll do my best . . .' Zoe's glancing at me. She must have caught me looking, and smiling, because she gives me a wave now, one of her classics, awkward and childlike, with her hand raised in front of her face as if to ward off a blow. I wave back. Though we aren't really standing that far apart; there's only the length of the phone cord between us, white and delicate and rippling like a charmed snake. Rippling more fiercely all of a sudden, then whipping the wall. What's this? Zoe's been miming something, and already I can hear the piano being played at your end – hear bright, loud shreds of music. Thank you, Simon, for taking her mind off that clown of a woman.

When Zoe showed me the letter this afternoon I tried to dampen her enthusiasm tactfully, without any crude spellings-out. 'Probably hopes to get material for a new comedy show, that's all,' I said.

But my girl's not that gullible any more. 'You're jealous,' she stated. Then, watching my face, she cried: 'Jealous! Jealous! Jealous!' and screamed with laughter, clapped her hands like an imp on the loose. In the end I was forced to use a pillow – gently, very gently – to silence her (not much point in alerting Ward Security over trifles, wouldn't you agree?). I knew she'd take it in her stride, and sure enough, once she'd calmed down she said in a perfectly reasonable voice (and with supreme disregard for my feelings):

'I wonder whether they'll let me wear my pink dress to meet Cara. You couldn't put in a word for me, could you?'

Later she was so excited she kept crossing and uncrossing her legs, didn't even stop after I'd squatted down by her side to redo the varnish on her toenails. It was hard not to grab hold of her, I admit, but experience has taught me a thing or two, and I've learnt to wait my turn. I contented myself with kneading her calves every so often, asking, 'That better?' solicitously – as if it was a mere case of jumpy legs.

When I'd got her relaxed enough I spoke up on your behalf, stressed how you were a man, and wouldn't she much rather have a man's attentions? 'Phone him again,' I said, 'to show you don't bear him a grudge, and send a photo as a follow-up.'

She giggled, then squeezed my shoulder, exclaiming: 'But I haven't even seen the pictures yet – you know, the ones you took outside!'

Listen, Simon, I don't think Zoe's enjoying your music any

longer. All that brashness must have worn her down; she stands crumpled against the wall, her foot has stopped tapping, and her eyes are filled with shadows.

So don't waste any more time now. Get on with the talking and leave the rest to me.

~

The arrangement works to perfection and Simon's glided into autopilot before he's halfway through Lesley's first solo. He can't but laugh at those ignorant off-the-cuff remarks Zoe had made recently, after he'd played her a short passage over the phone (without disclosing what it was, intending it as a test of sorts):

'I wish I could say I liked it better because you play it so well, Simon. But there's something in the music makes me go cold inside and out. Like the night Ralph locked me in the bathroom –'

Comparing his arrangement to a fucking bathroom – she was definitely not one of the talented ones, he told himself. Not having it in his heart to embarrass her, however, he merely let slip:

'"Bathroom music"! Weirdest comment about Saint-Saëns I've heard yet, must remember that one. Of course, he's –' 'an acquired taste' he was going on to say, but she'd keyed herself up into a desperate crescendo:

'Oh no, that's not what I meant, no, Simon!'

'No?'

'No, no! It's just – well, it reminded me of something that happened in our bathroom, long before the accident.'

She paused, and he shivered.

He'd hated her for using the word 'accident' in such a throwaway manner. Because for a moment she'd sent him back home again, a little boy: it's November once more, Miss Gleeson's been killed and there's that voice inside him, chafing him sore and raw, *'You've got what you wanted, got what you wanted, got what you wanted . . .'*

He kept shivering even after Zoe continued:

'Yes, long before. I was removing my make-up and day-dreaming. Ralph was waiting for me to come to bed. When I didn't appear straightaway, he flew into a temper. I finished up sleeping in the bath, wrapped in some towels. Next morning he apologised. And I forgave him. I was in love with him, wasn't I?' She checked herself then said hastily, 'Sorry, Simon, I hope you understand.'

Understanding hadn't come into it, not as far as he was concerned. He'd been trying to be nice, that was all, entertaining her (despite her ridiculous letter asking him to visit). So she hadn't enjoyed the passage he'd played to her? Hardly his fault. She still had a lot to learn.

Simon has reached the end of Lesley's solo and started on the next scene. His fingers have frozen into icicle points of precision, numb, no longer part of him. Playing like this is sheer delight, pure metaphysical delight . . . Was that the doorbell? Midday, and he isn't expecting anybody. He's got work to do. He carries on, but there it goes again, very distinctly this time. He launches into a *fortissimo*, puts in a bit of extra pedal work to slur over those rasping rings, then hammers away *forte fortissimo* right through the lovers' duet. The ringing doesn't stop.

~

Zoe's been clamouring for those pictures, Simon, claims she made an absolute fool of herself on the phone the other evening. They've come out well, especially the last one, snapped from the back, with her sitting on the bench after kicking the ground. I call it 'Seat of Punishment' – and rather aptly so – because seen against the dark threat of the trees in the background, the sharp-edged red slats cut across her like gashes. Not that *she* will ever set eyes on it, of course. What's mine's mine. I've already transferred it to my private portfolio – a bulging affair by now, and one of the well-deserved perks of some twenty-odd years in the service.

I spend hours in the company of my photos, laying out new ones, updating old ones with whatever titbits I've managed to dig up (I never leave a stone unturned, you might say, and the more wrigglies underneath the better), and gazing, simply gazing at those girls. To me, they're like so many crystal balls: I can see through clothes and hairstyles, behind mirrored glasses, I can see pasts, presents and futures, whether here, OUTSIDE or in some halfway house – once I glimpsed a nun's habit, and sure as fate, a couple of years later I heard the girl in question had taken the veil. Sometimes, sadly, freedom of choice is too much for them and we meet up again, true to my predictions.

Tomorrow I'll let Zoe have the pictures taken next to the fountain, though even *they* aren't entirely safe. Safe for general consumption, I mean. What with her having only one foot on the ground and one arm up in the air she looks pretty unbalanced, in dire need of protection; and the last thing I want is for other people to come rushing to her rescue.

Speak of the devil – There I was trying to finish my Progress Reports before going off duty when guess who should be put through on the external line? I knew her as soon as she opened her mouth – that stupid, salivating comic. Talked nineteen to the dozen: a pro all right and a bloody pain in the neck, excuse the language. She found her match, though.

Did Zoe like flowers? Oh, regulations. Velvet-soft African violets – no thorns, no harm, surely? No –? Well, OK. Sweets? Belgian chocolates quite delicious. No –? Video tapes, perhaps? Some recent sketches. Live footage. Hilarious. Might cheer her up. Anyway. Friday then. Visiting hours from. Yes. Fine. Thank you so much.

Positively wetting herself she was. But I've hatched a plot, and my boss owes me one for looking the other way on the ward a little while ago. Which only leaves you, Simon.

I'll help Zoe select a photo from the fountain series and offer to post it from OUTSIDE, to avoid red tape. Of course I won't send it off immediately; you must receive it on D-day, as it were. No doubt you'll find it hard to deal with the particular print I have in mind: Zoe frozen in action, unable to rid her memory of that fatal gesture, still flinging an imaginary hair dryer, over and over again. Or how about this, Simon: perhaps she'd like to throw something at *you*, smash it right through that high gloss finish, right into your face. Yes, how about it?

I'm sure you'll respond all the more nastily for feeling threatened. You just wait and see.

~

It's Mike who's been ringing the bell, and Simon feels oddly relieved. 'Sorry,' he shouts into the entry phone, 'didn't hear you!'

'Savaging that baby grand of yours again?' Mike's grin comes leaping up the last flight of stairs.

As he pulls the door closed, Simon wonders whether he's got the time for their rehearsal mixed up. He blames Zoe for his confusion – she's an easy scapegoat, after all. Then Mike says:

'I'm afraid you'll have to do without me today. One of the tenors in the Opera House chorus is ill, and yours truly's been asked to stand in. Have to be there for one. Sorry, man.'

But he doesn't look sorry at all; even his voice is grinning. Simon's happy for him (and for himself, of course, thinking in terms of CVs and his Saint-Saëns project):

'Sounds great. Though I *had* hoped –' pointing at the carrier bag in Mike's hand, '– to see the Samson hairdo ... We'll have to toast your good fortune instead.' He squeezes past the table into the kitchen and returns with two glasses and a bottle: 'Monday OK for our next rehearsal? Say half four?'

'Fine.' Mike's fingering the golden label and ribbon

appreciatively: '"Amarula – wild fruit cream." Exotic stuff that. But just a drop for me, thanks.'

'From one of my well-heeled students.' He chuckles and pours while Mike moves the pile of newspapers to one side – only to reveal something small and shiny underneath. That bloody picture! Simon knows he'll have to act fast now, play it cool and understated, like a little Haydn number. So when Mike jokes about private centrefolds he says carelessly:

'Oh, her? She's been hassling me with phone calls and letters for ages.' He reaches for the photo: '*This* came today – and is going straight out again.'

Zoe's seaweed eyes seem to shiver away from him – a crack in the gloss, no doubt – and to focus on the wall behind. Quickly he rips her in half, rips up the halves, then the halves of the halves till nothing remains but a scatter of fuzzy confetti. That'll teach her! Still, part of him feels a twinge of regret. Or fear.

Mike's shaking his head, 'God's sake, man, that's like sticking pins into a doll.'

'She'll survive, don't worry.' Simon laughs, almost persuading himself, and raises his glass: 'Cheers!'

~

D-day at last, Simon. That picture should have arrived by now. First delivery. As for the rest, I'll just have to take my chances. But don't you forget: whatever happens, Zoe belongs to *me*.

'A surprise!' I greeted her when I opened the cell door this morning. 'Change into your OUTSIDE clothes, hurry! You don't want to waste time hanging around here!' Then I took a step towards her, lifting my arms as if for an embrace, though really to show off my new flame-pink skirt, very tight and elegant and bought specially for the occasion (after all, Zoe'd never yet seen me out of my drab and baggy guard's clothes).

She didn't move. Stiffly she stood where she was near

the window, the shadows of its bars like hands upon her, her hothouse beauty stripped to a harshness of bone under petal-thin skin.

'Zoe,' I whispered and went and parted the still air in front of her face with my fingers, trying to unweave the spell: 'Day release, Zoe, you're free for the day. Free!'

We set off about an hour ago and knowing her, she'll want to call you any moment now. So be warned. We're travelling in my private car: no handcuffs or other policing gadgets, just a mobile phone, a box of chocolates and a few Reggae cassettes, the latter a compromise (I have to confess I hate classical stuff even more when I'm driving). Our trip has gone well so far and we've shared some of the chocolates, with her feeding me one at a time like I asked her. Except that I once mistook her fingers for the real thing and that she's started to cross and uncross her legs again, which makes concentrating on the road rather difficult.

'I've staked my reputation on this, Zoe,' I'd told her earlier, after I convinced her it *was* true, and yes, we *were* going to visit you. 'Promise to do as I say?'

'Yes, yes!' She'd been close to tears and slid up to me half-naked (nothing improper about that, you understand: she was in the middle of getting changed).

And now she's wearing her favourite pink dress and matching court shoes, no make-up because I prefer her without – she looks younger that way and brings out the best in people, like a little bird without feathers. She's crossed and uncrossed her legs so often her skin's begun to slap and suck damply whenever she moves (I can hear it even above the engine noise and the music). And every time I change gear I seem to brush against her knee. I wish I'd kissed her in the cell before. Not passionately, not like that evening she was playing the piano, but quiet and slow, as if she was mine already, with my lips flickering all over her face, feeling her eyelashes tremble and her blood pulse in her throat.

The last few chords of 'No Woman, No Cry' are fading in my ears when Zoe touches me on the shoulder:

'We'll be there soon. May I ring him now to see if he's in?' A pause. 'But what if he isn't? I shall go crazy, crazy, crazy . . .'

Smiling inwardly, I say to myself: 'Oh no you won't, my dear. Not unless it's "crazy" for me . . .' Then, aloud, I reassure her in my most calming guard's tone, 'Don't worry, Zoe. It's only just past noon, and I've got this feeling that things'll work out. Trust me.'

Another suck-and-slap and she's half-kneeling in her seat, leaning towards me till her breath's crinkling up against my face; she's a quick learner, my little girl, primed for the finals, as it were . . .

'All right, all right. On you go – You know what to say, don't you? And remember: no messages. You can try again later.'

Her hands are fumbling for the mobile on my lap.

Now, Simon, you'd better be ready.

~

They're still savouring their Amarula when the phone starts to ring. 'Lesley,' Simon thinks, a trifle guilty, and arms his voice with a smile: 'Hello?'

After the slightest of hesitations someone shouts, 'You're in, thank God!', and it takes him a second to recognise her now that she isn't whispering.

'Simon, guess what: I'm on day release! I'd love to come and see you. Just for a short while, please, Simon.'

'Oh, hi Zoe.' He puts a hand over the mouthpiece, nods towards the table: 'That damn girl again,' but Mike's about to slip away, discreet as anything, with a suave little flick of his wrist. Simon gestures for him to stay; he can't let him leave now, not yet. He means to hang up – he doesn't want her and her 'accident' in the flat, reminding him; he doesn't want her, period. Instead he hears himself lapse into the old Mr-Nice-Guy mode:

'This afternoon? Actually, I'd planned to go out. Pity ... What time exactly were you thinking of?'

There's a strange crackling noise on the line, then she cries, breathless with excitement: 'I'm in town already. Say in about quarter of an hour? And thanks, Simon, thanks a million!'

The phone's gone dead. Through the window he catches sight of a bright yellow pram being wheeled along the other side of the street, its hood a sweaty glare in the sun – all these mothers with their babies, trundling up and down like they've nothing better to do. When he turns, Mike's already by the door:

'Two's company ... Anyway, I really must be off, Simon. Thanks for the drink.' From the landing outside follows a hasty farewell wave: 'Apologies to Lesley, and – good luck!'

Afterwards Simon sweeps up the confetti. Then he just stands there. He feels stuck. Like the square of white sky in the kitchen window, stuck and empty. Waiting for something to happen. Lesley seems far away all of a sudden; she belongs to another time zone, another world. A world without vicious circles, without whisper voices. He is that small boy again, hoping the ring at the door won't come. Only *this* time he knows it will.

The church clock round the corner strikes the half-hour. She'll be here any minute, there's no stopping her. Except that his fingers have begun to itch and throb and pull as if at a secret command. They draw him towards the baby grand. They hit the keys full force, springing them like mines. Welding him to Baba Yaga's hellfire rhythms. Over and over. The same few lines, same few bars, same few chords ...

When the doorbell rings he won't pay any attention, and if she should start shouting, well – who cares? He'll just keep playing. Play the guilt away, and the bewitchings. Play Miss Gleeson away. Play Zoe away. They have nothing to do with him, he nothing with them. The piano is all they've ever had in common, and that's meaningless enough. Millions of people could say the same.

~

'Jungle music. I'd have him locked up if I was his neighbour,' I can't help remarking. But then, this isn't exactly the most desirable part of town, is it, Simon? Pubs with pretty names and scabby, bloated walls, front gardens covered in dog shit and garbage, and that rubbery squelch of the traffic over the cobbles.

'Mussorgsky,' Zoe says after ringing the bell, her head thrown back as if to bask in that noise of yours thumping out from one of the upstairs windows. 'No wonder he can't hear us. But he'll be finished soon; this is Baba Yaga, the witch's piece, the second last. He knows I'm coming.'

Ever the romantic, isn't she? Even I can tell you've been repeating yourself. And it doesn't sound like you're practising either.

There's an empty glass bottle next to some vegetable peels by the railings, simply begging to be shuffled about. Every time it rolls over the patch of dried mud between my feet it gives a kind of gritty shriek.

I hope I can count on you not to answer the door, Simon. That was merely your good manners talking on the phone, wasn't it? Because I'm sure you don't really want to meet her, not after all these weeks of never acknowledging her, never responding to any of her letters or calls. I wouldn't like to have to make a scene dragging and hustling and screaming her away from you in public. Which is precisely what I will do if –

And that's the bottle wobbling into the gutter, still intact.

Zoe's getting a little restless. She's just pushed your bell again, her third attempt, longer and harder than before, whiter knuckled, her face more strained-looking.

'Bastard. Bastard. Lying bastard.' Swearing under her breath now, what a naughty girl.

Well done, Simon, or rather, *not* done. Everything's going according to plan, and this is the moment to put my arms round her, then lead her back to the car, tightening my grip ever so slightly, perhaps risking one of the phrases I've prepared: 'He isn't worth it, Zoe. Not worth one line on the palm of your hand.'

Instead, I find myself gazing at the bottle nearby. It has stopped wobbling; its whole length is glinting with intent now, right up to the twisted, thin-lipped mouth. It's telling me to pick it up if I've got any sense.

Which I have, of course. And so, holding the thing by the neck, I start to swing it to and fro. Like a pendulum – to and fro, to and fro, to and fro – or a missile in disguise. To and fro. To and fro. Zoe's broken off in mid-'bastard' and is watching me, a captive audience quite literally. And that's what we want, isn't it, Simon? No thinking, not till afterwards. Just a reflex, a pure reflex action: her snatching the bottle and hurling it into one of those windows, hurling it like it's a hair dryer and the window her lover, a ghost to be killed one last time.

Needless to say, it'll be me who'll get her out of here, quick as magic, before anyone has a chance to ask questions. All for her sake, naturally. You'll be rid of her, Simon, and she'll be mine, guilty and grateful – very, very grateful. I swing the bottle towards her, squint up into the sunlight at what must be your window. Swing and squint. Swing and squint. Zoe's coming closer. A moth drawn to the flame. Swing and squint. Then it bumps against her hip and she goes rigid, stares me full in the face. Reflected in her eyes I see a bird streak past, like the shadow of a memory.

Now, Simon, now. If ever there was a spellbinding moment, this is it. Her hand will reach out for the bottle, tug it free. Her fingers will lock round it, her arm lift back, and she'll let go. She'll have to.

When I feel her take it I pretend not to notice, turning my head towards the car parked further up the street, and waiting – she'll be mine at long, long last, *mine* — waiting for the smash of a window, whether yours or whoever's doesn't really matter.

But this sounds different, not a window shattering; much shorter, sharper. Someone screams — a woman. A young woman with a yellow pram, and there's glass all over it. And blood.

'Why don't you look where you're going!' I yell. My voice cuts her silent. What a stupid bitch, pushing that pram of hers straight into an accident. An accident. Yes. That's all it is. My poor girl trapped into an accident. The spell broken, just like that. Broken. No more action replays now to make her safe. Ghosts all round her. Even her baby was killed.

She's crossed over to the other side. Kicked off her shoes. Running.

'Zoe! Wait for me! Zoeeeeee!'

She keeps running. Away from the car. The distance between us lengthening. I'll have to catch her. Mustn't let her out of my sight. I mustn't. Mustn't. Mustn't. She's mine. My own little girl.

The piano is still being played. The woman has started screaming again, a high-pitched wail like a siren. Getting fainter fast.

When I look over my shoulder, several cars have pulled up and people are gathering round her and the pram. She'll be held and patted and comforted. She'll be safe all right. And the baby. Safe as safe can be.

I hurry after Zoe. The jungle music is growing louder, inside my head.

~

Other similar titles from Scottish Cultural Press

Special Deliverance: short stories
Donald S Murray
1 898218 99 4

Night Visits
Ron Butlin
1 84017 000 X

The Summer is Ended
Kenneth C Steven
1 898218 72 2

Contact the publishers direct for a complete catalogue
and further information